Hugo was much too strong to resist

"You're not getting away from me again," he promised Kate grimly. He was standing over her, pinning her to the wall by her shoulders, his face, dark and angry, only a few inches away from her own. Kate stared back, her eyes wide with fright.

"Yes, you're right to be afraid, because I've several scores to settle with you. But first, you're going to do some talking."

"You can ask all the questions you want," she said in a trembling but defiant voice, "but I won't answer you. I just want to be free of you!"

"Sit down!" he said coldly. "Now you know I can force you to do anything I want. So you'll sit there and you'll answer any question I put to you, do you understand?"

SALLY
WENTWORTH

shattered dreams

Harlequin Books

TORONTO • NEW YORK • LONDON
AMSTERDAM • PARIS • SYDNEY • HAMBURG
STOCKHOLM • ATHENS • TOKYO • MILAN

Harlequin Presents first edition September 1983
ISBN 0-373-10629-7

Original hardcover edition published in 1979
by Mills & Boon Limited

Printed in U.S.A.

CHAPTER ONE

IT was one of the most fashionable London Society weddings of the year. Everyone was there: the rich and titled relations of the groom, the modishly dressed friends of the bride; and the housewives who had gathered outside the gates of the church were having a high old time trying to guess the identities of the various guests.

'Ooh, I recognise 'er,' one said excitedly as she nudged her companion. 'She's a model like the bride. She was on the cover of my women's magazine last week. Ain't she lovely?'

'Not as nice as the bride, though,' her neighbour returned. 'Don't she look a picture? That dress must have cost a small fortune. Not that the groom can't afford it. I read in the paper that he's almost a millionaire as well as being an Honourable!'

The bride and groom came nearer and the first woman said somewhat wistfully, 'The groom's ever so good-looking. Bit stern, but I'd swap my Bert for 'im any day.'

'They say she's only marrying him for his money,' her friend rejoined.

'Well, I don't know what she's marrying him for, but I know darn well what he's marrying her for!'

They chuckled together as the bridal couple passed them and got into a Rolls-Royce which whisked them away to the reception at the Hyde Park Hotel.

As the bride settled back into her seat, the creamy lace of her veil thrown back to outline the fine-boned, classic beauty of her face, she glanced back at the two chattering women. Their last remark had been pitched loud enough for her to hear as she passed them, and it had brought a slight flush to her pale cheeks. She tried not to resent the remark, knowing that it was made in ignorance, tried not to let it mar the great well of happiness deep inside her, happiness that she was almost afraid to display and acknowledge. It all seemed so unreal still, as if it wasn't truly happening to her, as if she was moving through a wonderful dream and that any minute she might wake and find herself back in a world where there was no car, no wedding, no Hugo.

She turned to look at him then and found him watching her quizzically. He looked so suave and elegant in his morning suit, but then he always carried whatever clothes he was wearing with an easy grace, his broad shoulders and his height, together with his years of training as a Guards officer, giving him a quietly commanding, authoritative air that made him stand out from the crowd. Tremulously she smiled at him and Hugo raised her left hand with the bright new wedding ring on it to his lips, his long-lashed grey eyes never leaving hers.

It still seemed unbelievable. She didn't think she'd ever get used to no longer being plain Kate Selby. Mrs Katherine Merrion, wife of the Honourable Hugo Merrion. The new name sounded like that of a stranger she had just met and needed time to get to know.

But it was no time at all before they were at the hotel and the doorman was rushing to help her out.

Several people were waiting to greet them in the first of the suite of rooms set aside for the reception and Kate answered them with her lovely, professional smile that had brightened the covers of thousands of magazines during her modelling career, a career that she was now giving up at Hugo's insistence. She had expected to stay in the room to welcome the guests arriving from the church, but Hugo said a firm, 'Excuse me' to everyone and took her elbow to lead her into another, empty room where all the wedding gifts had been put on display. There were a great many of them, ranging from a solid silver tea-service, through the inevitable duplication of crystal decanters, to a set of table-mats.

Hugo's hold on her arm tightened and he turned her round to face him. Kate's heart began to pound wildly as he put his hand up to gently caress her face.

'Oh, Kate, how lovely you are. *La plus belle Katherine du monde*,' he quoted softly, his eyes exploring for the thousandth time the perfect beauty of her features as his fingers outlined the curve of her cheek. His mouth came down to seek her own, his lips firm and demanding as the kiss became deeper and he held her close against him. 'Oh, my darling,' he said huskily, 'I can't wait to get you to myself.'

Trembling with emotion, Kate could only cling to him wordlessly, a great flood of happiness and desire filling her as she gazed mistily up at the dark handsomeness of his face. She loved him so much, sometimes she thought she would burst with the intensity of her feelings for him. And to know that he loved her in return! It was like having prayed for a miracle and to have it granted. Incredible, unbelievable, but true. Hugo bent to kiss her again, but there was a discreet tap at the door and someone told them that the first of the guests were arriving.

After that there was no more time to be alone together, but the memory of those snatched few minutes sustained Kate through the next hour of greeting aristocratic strangers who were related to Hugo, his business friends, ex-fellow Guards officers and their wives, old school friends, fellow club members—the list seemed endless. But among them were her own friends from the fashion world: her agent, some photographers and editors, and several of her fellow models who greeted her exuberantly. Marked among the guests was the absence of any close relations on Kate's side as she was an orphan, but, as Hugo had remarked, he had more than enough for both of them. But Kate wished heartily that her one relation, an older half-brother, had been here to give her moral support, but he was now halfway round the world, his attempt to attend the wedding thwarted at the last minute by a crisis in his job.

Hugo's friends and relations were overtly pleasant towards her, but with her nerves at their most sensitive, Kate was aware of an unspoken undercurrent because she wasn't one of them. She was one of the common herd who was acceptable only because of the beauty that made her stand out from the crowd, someone who could be tolerated even more because she had no close relations who could be a possible source of embarrassment.

The talk and laughter of the guests rose in volume proportionate to the amounts of vintage champagne that flowed freely, no expense spared, and soon she was laughingly helping Hugo to cut the four-tiered wedding cake with his Army sword, he was replying eloquently and wittily to the toasts, and then, thank heaven, it was time for them to go and change for the long flight to the Bahamas where they were to spend their honeymoon.

A couple of her friends came up with her to one of the bedrooms of the suite on the fourth floor that Hugo had engaged for their use. The girls helped her to change out of her wedding gown and into an amber-coloured dress with a matching jacket. Then she laughingly protested that she could manage alone and shooed them out before she went into the bathroom that lay between her room and the one Hugo was using to change in. She looked in the mirror with professional criticism, dispassionately examining each feature of her carefully made-up face: the finely arched brows over the amber-flecked green eyes, the perfect straightness of her nose and her well-shaped mouth with just the hint of hidden sensuality in her lower lip. Her hair, that rare shade between red and gold, was drawn back from her face and she decided to leave it as it was, the style adding sophistication to her twenty-two years.

It was as she was leaning forward to apply fresh lipstick that she heard the sound of men's voices and realised that the communicating door between the bathroom and Hugo's room was ajar. She recognised Hugo's voice and that of Adam Ralston, his best man and closest friend. Unhurriedly she blotted her lipstick and then went to close the door, but Hugo's raised voice caused her to stand transfixed, her hand still holding the door knob.

'The bitch! The dirty, cheating little bitch! And to think I was fool enough to let her trap me into marrying her!'

Kate felt as if she'd been kicked in the stomach and couldn't have moved if she'd tried. The beating of her heart, the gentle sigh of her breath, all seemed still as she listened agonisingly for what came next. He couldn't be talking about her, he couldn't! It must be someone else.

'Hold hard, Hugo,' Adam's voice cut in. 'You've only this one piece of evidence to go on.'

'My God, what more do I need? The detective agency not only give details of this man staying overnight at her flat, but say that there's evidence to prove he's stayed there for various lengths of time for several years. And there's a photostat of the sale of her flat showing that he paid for it and installed her there. And to cap it all there's a photograph of her with the man taken in the early hours of yesterday morning— yesterday morning, mark you, Adam. Look, they're kissing one another goodbye in the doorway of her flat.' His voice became a contemptuous snarl. 'You'll notice she's wearing nothing but a nightdress.'

There was a short silence in which only the sound of Hugo's feet as he savagely paced the floor could be heard. Then Adam said reluctantly, 'It certainly looks pretty bad. Who is this chap?'

'His name's Leo Crawford. I've never heard of him, have you?'

But Kate didn't listen to the reply; she sank back against the wall as realisation dawned and with it a relief that suddenly brought life back to her numbed senses. For Leo Crawford was her half-brother. He had

arrived unexpectedly in London from Buenos Aires
for the wedding two days ago, much to Kate's delight,
but early the following morning, when he was still
sleeping off his jet-lag, his company had recalled him
urgently to cope with a crisis that only he could deal
with. And she hadn't seen Hugo since to tell him of it.
The relief that it was all a stupid mistake was for a
moment overwhelming and Kate took a little time to
regain her composure before she went in to Hugo to
tell him.

'What made you put a detective on to her in the first
place?' Adam was asking.

'It was my aunt; she kept on at me that Kate
couldn't possibly be as innocent as she made herself out
to be. Then she said she'd heard rumours of another
man. It was to prove her wrong as much as anything
that I hired the detective. And there was nothing until
now. The slut must have thought herself safe because
I was holding my stag party.'

'The report was waiting for you here?'

'Yes, it must have got mixed up with the wedding
telegrams. If only I'd received it just a few hours
earlier!'

'You wouldn't have called off the wedding?' Adam's
voice sounded startled.

'Yes, I damn well would!' Hugo answered vehemently. 'Don't you realise what that girl did, Adam?
She made me believe that she was as clean and good on
the inside as she was lovely on the outside. I wanted
her, Adam. I still want her more than I've ever wanted
a woman. And I married her because I thought it was
the only way I could get her!'

The walls of the bathroom seemed to sway and spin

wildly round her and Kate clung to the towel rail, gripping it tightly as she strove to stop herself from fainting, the happy dream beginning to turn into a nightmare.

'Well, even if she isn't everything you thought her, you've still got her,' Adam was pointing out.

'Oh, yes,' Hugo's voice was sharp with bitter irony. 'I've got her all right—still warm from another man's bed!'

'What are you going to do? The fact that she was living with another man isn't sufficient grounds for having the marriage annulled, you know.'

'I don't want it annulled. That little slut's made a fool out of me, Adam, and by God I'm going to make her pay for it!'

'How?'

There was a short silence and then Kate could almost imagine the fierce, violent anger in Hugo's face as he replied curtly, 'She's obviously marrying me for only two things: money, of course, and the social position I can give her. Well, it will be quite easy to keep her out of society, to have the door slammed in her face and keep her in her place, and as for money—it's going to be the other way round. Marrying her has been an expensive business and I'm going to make sure that I get my money's worth out of her before I kick her back into the gutter where she belongs!'

Any thoughts that Kate had had about walking in there and telling him the truth had now died completely. She was absolutely shattered by what she had heard. To learn that his professed feelings for her were nothing but a hollow sham, that he had married her only because he had wanted her so much sexually that he would do anything to get her, was like the final knock-out blow after a series of cruel punches. She felt literally sick and had to lean her burning forehead against the smooth coolness of the tiled wall, her hands over her ears to cut out the blows he was inflicting on her. But when she took her hands away they were still discussing her.

'She put on this virtuous act from the day we met,' Hugo was explaining furiously. 'I tried to take her to bed, of course, even offered to set her up as my mistress.' He gave a short, savage laugh. 'But she was playing for higher stakes. She'd look at me with that sort of hurt innocence in her eyes and I—God help me, I believed her when she said she wasn't that type of girl. I'm surprised she didn't take up acting instead of modelling, she'd have been a roaring success,' he added with a snarl.

The sound of his voice came nearer and Kate turned her head to see him framed by the small gap between the door and the wall. He was still wearing his grey morning suit, the white carnation still in his buttonhole, but his face was bleak, his eyes dark with murderous rage. His words carried to her quite clearly. 'I wonder just how the bitch intended to pass herself off as a virgin on our wedding night—or did she think that I'd be so besotted by then that I wouldn't care? But I'm going to make sure she pays, Adam, pays and keeps on paying until that lying little slut begs me to let her go!'

Unable to bear any more, Kate moved silently out of the bathroom and into her room, softly turning the key in the lock behind her. She looked unseeingly round the room, unable to take in anything but the white lace wedding dress spread out across the bed waiting to be carefully packed and stored away, a remembrance of what should have been the happiest day of her life. Her senses were too numb for her to cry, too bruised for her to think clearly. Aimlessly she wandered to the mirror and stared at herself. How could she still look the same, why didn't the misery that filled her make her look different, like a different person? Because that was what she was, an entirely changed girl from the one who had walked so happily into this room less than half an hour ago.

Something caught her eye and she glanced down to see her new leather handbag on the dressing table, the one that she had bought especially to match her going-away outfit. Abstractedly she picked it up and began to fiddle with the clasp, her mind a desperate jumble as she tried to think what she was going to do. The only thing she did know, and that with utmost certainty, was that she never wanted to see Hugo again. He had turned what she had thought to be a loving, trusting relationship into a dirty, degraded thing, had taken it for granted that she was as mercenary as he, that she must be as greedy for money and position as he was greedy to own and possess her sexually. Gradually the misery in her heart began to change to bitter, hopeless anger. He'd made it very clear what he had in store for her, but Kate didn't intend to stay around to let him take his vengeance out on her. And she certainly didn't intend to go to the bother of explaining, proving that he was wrong about her, because even that didn't matter now. His words had shown that he didn't really care about her. He had made everything between them cheap and sordid, when all the time she'd been so....

But that didn't bear thinking about. Not yet. Not for a long time. Now all she must do was to think how to get out of this mess as quickly as possible.

She flicked the clasp of her bag again and it came open, her passport nestling inside where she had put it for safe keeping, intending to give it to Hugo when they reached the airport. With all the fuss and excitement of the wedding she had forgotten that she needed to get it changed to her new name until it was too late to do so. Kate looked across the room to where her new set of matching suitcases stood ready packed with all the clothes she had bought for her trousseau; expensive clothes because she hadn't wanted to let Hugo down, and which she had insisted on paying for herself although they had cost nearly every penny she possessed, for she had been too proud to let Hugo pay for them as he had offered to. The thought made her mouth curl bitterly for a moment, but she resolutely pulled her thoughts back to the present. Then her eyes slowly widened as she realised that all her things were here, there was nothing to stop her just walking out of the hotel, out of Hugo's life!

Without giving herself time to think about the enormity of what she was doing, what the guests might think or of what a scandal it would cause, Kate picked up the telephone and asked for a taxi to be ready for her at the side entrance of the hotel and also for a porter to be sent up to collect her luggage. The key to her vanity case was in her purse and she quickly unlocked it and took out three jewellery boxes containing a pearl necklace that Hugo had given her as an engagement present, the diamond bracelet and earrings that he had given her only a few days ago as a wedding present, and a small, rather lovely brooch in the shape of a butterfly that she had admired in a shop and he had immediately insisted on buying for her, so that afterwards she had been careful never to express a liking for anything again in case he might think her a gold-digger.

Dropping the boxes on top of the wedding dress, Kate slowly took off the diamond and sapphire spray engagement ring and then the thick, bright wedding band, letting them fall from her fingers to lie on the rich white satin and lace. She wanted nothing that he had given her, she just wanted to get away, to be free of him.

When the porter rapped at the door she was able to greet him calmly and quietly and to follow him from the room without a backward glance.

There were a harrowing few minutes as she walked down the corridor and waited for the lift, but the side entrance was on the floor below the rooms in which the reception was being held and she made it without seeing anyone who looked even vaguely familiar. The porter put her cases in the waiting taxi, she remembered to give him a generous tip, and then the door slammed shut.

The driver turned to her. 'Where to, miss?'

For a few minutes she couldn't think, could only stare at him blankly; she hadn't given a thought to where she was going, had been completely oblivious to everything except the need to get away. 'Could—could you just drive around for a while, please?'

The man looked at her in surprise, then shrugged and turned on his meter before pulling into the stream of noisy traffic. Thankfully Kate leaned back in the seat as she watched the façade of the hotel disappear through the window. No one had seen her, she had got clean away. The taxi pulled into Hyde Park and drove sedately down the tree-lined avenue. She would have liked to just lie back and let her brain go numb, but she couldn't drive around indefinitely, she had to think what she was going to do. That she couldn't go back to her flat was quite certain; it would be the first place Hugo would look for her, and she had no doubts that once he found out she had run away he would come after her, intent on taking the revenge he thought due to him. So where else could she go? She had no relatives except Leo. She supposed that if it came to it she could join him in Buenos Aires, but she didn't have enough money left to get there and it would probably take some days for her to cable Leo and for him to transfer some money to her bank. And she might need a special visa to go to Argentina for all she knew. Wretchedly she looked out at the strollers in the park, wondering what on earth she was going to do. She had plenty of friends who would put her up for a while, but they were all at the reception, and besides, Hugo knew them all and could check to see if she was with them.

Worriedly she wondered if she ought to see a lawyer, find out what she had to do to keep Hugo away from her. There must be some sort of law that.... Her thoughts flew off at a tangent. Of course—Margie! Why hadn't she thought of her before? Margie Robertson was one of her oldest friends, they had started modelling at the same time, but Margie had married over three years ago and gone to live with her solicitor husband in North London. Kate had, of course, invited them to the wedding, but Margie's twin boys, her godsons, had been unwell and they hadn't been able to attend. And she was quite sure that Hugo had never met them. Leaning forward, she tapped on the glass and gave the driver the address. She would be safe at Margie's, Hugo would never be able to find her there.

There was a little delay after she had rung the bell of the pleasant suburban house in Hendon, a delay in which Kate waited with mounting panic. Suppose Margie wasn't in, what could she do? But then her rather harassed-looking friend came to the door, her mouth dropping open in astonishment when she saw who it was.

'Kate! But—but aren't you supposed to be ...?' She shook her head in bewilderment. 'I'm sorry, I must have got the date wrong. I could have sworn you were getting married today.'

'I—I did,' Kate faltered. 'Oh, Margie, please let me come in. I—I've left him!' And she suddenly began to laugh and cry hysterically at the ridiculousness of what she'd said.

Somehow she found herself pulled inside and her cases stacked in the hall, then she was pushed into a settee in the sitting-room and a glass of whisky put in her hand.

'Here, drink this,' Margie ordered. 'Hang on for two minutes while I get the kids settled and I'll be right down.'

When she came back Kate was still crying, but the first great flood of tears was over and she was able to relate what had happened without becoming hysterical again.

Margie just sat and stared at her when she had finished. 'You mean you just walked out of the reception? Without a word?'

Silently Kate nodded.

'Good for you!' Margie got up and started pacing the room. 'But first you should have gone in there and told him what you thought of him, told him what he could do with his money and his position! The skunk! I always knew you were too good for him, and this proves it. I told the others they were out of their minds when they said you were marrying him for what you could get out of him, and this....' She stopped abruptly. 'Sorry, Kate, I shouldn't have said that.'

Leaning back tiredly against the settee, Kate said dully, 'It doesn't matter. People always believe the worst. Can I stay here for a bit, Margie? Till I decide what I'm going to do?'

'Of course you can, you don't have to ask. You must stay as long as you like.' Her friend came to sit beside her and patted her hand comfortingly. 'Try not to take it too hard, love. We'll work it out somehow. You did the right thing when you walked out on him.' One of the twins began to cry and she lifted her head worriedly to listen. 'Oh, darn, there he goes again!'

'I'm sorry,' Kate apologised. 'I should have asked you how the babies were before. Aren't they any better?'

'No, they seem worse. I've called the doctor again and he should be here any time now. It's some sort of throat infection.'

'You go to them,' Kate urged. 'I'm all right, really.'

'Sure you don't mind?'

'No, you go ahead. I'll make myself a coffee.'

While Margie hurried upstairs, Kate went slowly to the kitchen and filled the percolator. She still felt punch-drunk, bemused by what had happened and unable to think straight, unwilling to even contemplate the future that loomed bleak and empty before her. Why on earth had she been so blind? Why couldn't she have seen that Hugo's feelings for her were all a pretence, an act he'd put on to get what he wanted? But an act so good that she had been convinced that he loved her.

She was still standing at the sink, staring blindly down, when Margie found her.

'Look, love, I'm going to call Simon, tell him about this. Come and sit down.' She picked up the receiver of the wall phone and called her husband, asking him to come home after telling him what had happened. Putting the phone down, she turned to where Kate was sitting listlessly at the table and said, 'He's coming straightaway. He'll only be about twenty minutes.' She went on talking to Kate, trying to comfort her, but all the time she was nervy and on edge, and when the doorbell rang she jumped up quickly, relief on her face. 'Thank goodness, that must be the doctor.'

Margie hurried away and took the doctor upstairs to the twins' room. They were gone a long time. Simon came in before they came down and gave her such a comforting hug that she almost burst into tears again. She and Simon had known each other for many years, having lived in the same town in Somerset, and he had looked her up when he came to work in London, but from the moment she had introduced him to Margie there had been no one else for him. Kate had been a bridesmaid at their wedding and was used to looking on him not only as a friend but also as an adviser over contracts and any other legal matters that arose about her work.

He said now, 'Try not to let it upset you too much,

Kate. It seems a hell of a mess now, I know, but we'll sort it out, you'll see.'

'He can't make me go back to him, can he?' she asked anxiously.

'Not if you don't want to. But you should let him know where you are, because he might. . . .'

'No!' Kate broke in vehemently. 'You mustn't tell him where I am. He'll drag me back, I know he will. You didn't hear him, Simon. He was so furious that he threatened to make me pay, to get his money's worth out of me.'

Her voice had risen hysterically and Simon hastily broke in to reassure her. 'All right, Kate, don't worry about it now. We'll work something out.'

He got her a mug of coffee and laced it with whisky, making her drink it strong and hot. The mug had a green hippopotamus on it, she noticed inconsequentially. Margie joined them soon after that, a troubled frown on her face.

'The doctor says they'll probably be unwell and fretful for a couple of days yet before the infection clears up, and he's told me to keep them in separate rooms so that they don't wake each other up. So it looks as if we're in for a couple of disturbed nights,' she told them.

Kate said at once, 'In that case you won't want me around. I'll only add to your worries. I'll find a hotel or something.'

Immediately Simon answered, 'Don't be silly. You can sleep with Margie and I'll go in with one of the twins.'

'No, I'll only be in the way. And thanks to you I'm over the worst. I'll be all right on my own now, honestly,' Kate replied with a firmness she was far from feeling.

They tried to dissuade her, saying that she'd be no trouble, but Kate knew how worried they must be about the children and was adamant in refusing to add to the burden.

'But where would you go?' Margie objected.

'I don't know. As far away as possible. Anywhere so long as Hugo doesn't find me. I—I just can't cope with facing him.'

'Kate, are you absolutely sure that there's no hope of you getting together? If he asks for a reconciliation. . . .'

'No. He's killed everything that was between us— that I thought was between us,' she corrected herself painfully. 'Okay, he might ask for a reconciliation, but only because he still wants me. And when he's had enough of me he'll kick me out.' She raised her eyes, their green depths heavy with unhappiness. 'He said so, Simon. Those were his exact words.'

'All right. But as your solicitor I think that I should write to him and tell him that you want the marriage annulled at once. Your refusal to consummate the marriage is grounds enough for that. I won't tell him where you are,' he added when he saw that she was about to object. 'I'll simply tell him that you've instructed me to act for you. Then I'll contact you as soon as he replies.'

Kate eventually agreed to this, but still couldn't decide where to go. 'Perhaps I'll take a train up to Scotland or somewhere in the north. I can let you know the address when I find some place to stay.' She had an overwhelming urge to get as far away from Hugo as possible.

'Wait a minute,' Margie interrupted suddenly, click-ing her fingers as inspiration hit her. 'Why can't you go and stay at the villa?'

'Of course,' Simon agreed at once. 'It would be ideal. You remember, Kate; we invested our all into an old farm in Majorca and spent all our holidays before the twins came in modernising it. You'll be safe enough from Hugo Merrion there and you can stay until you make up your mind what you want to do. You'll only need to buy your food and we've got a car there if you want to get around and explore a bit. What do you say?'

'Majorca? Well, I suppose I could. I've got my pass-port and enough money for my fare. Yes,' she gave a tremulous smile. 'Yes, I think I'd like that.'

'Sure you won't mind being on your own?' Margie asked.

'No, I think I'd prefer it really. As Simon said, it will give me time to think.'

'I'll ring the airport and book you a flight,' Simon offered.

He managed to get her a seat on a flight leaving at seven that evening which just gave them time to have a hasty meal before they left for the airport, Simon in-sisting on driving her. Kate took a hurried but warm farewell of Margie and promised to write and let them know that she'd arrived safely, then they were speeding to the airport and Simon was pushing a luggage trolley up to the airline desk for her.

'You'll have to get a taxi from Palma airport to the farm, I'm afraid. Look, Margie said you'd spent most of your cash, so I want you to take this, you might need it.' He thrust a bundle of notes into her hand. Kate tried to protest and give it back to him, but he insisted she take it. 'Pay it back when you're working again,' he told her, and in the end she accepted gratefully. He walked her to the door of the Departure Lounge and turned her round to grip her shoulders tightly. 'And remember, just because one man has let you down, turned out to be a swine, it doesn't mean that it's the end of the world.' He gave her a slight shake, his face full of concern for her. 'You're not to do anything crazy, do you understand? He's not worth it. Just think yourself darn lucky that you found out in time. And stop trying to bottle it all up. I'll get you an annulment and then you can put all this behind you. Now promise me you'll be sensible about this, or I'll break your arm.'

Kate managed a weak grin. 'Okay, Simon, I promise.'

'Good.' He pulled her gently to him and kissed her on the forehead in his familiar and friendly way. 'I'll write to you as soon as there's any news.' He gave her a little push towards the doors. 'Your flight's being called. Off you go.'

As the plane took off she caught a last glimpse of his solid, dependable figure waving to her from the roof of the airport building and when he disappeared from sight she felt a sense of loss that was almost as great as she had sustained earlier that day.

There was no difficulty in getting a taxi at Palma, but it took nearly an hour to drive inland across the island to the villa. Gradually the blocks of hotels and apartment buildings gave way to ordinary houses and shops and then to the occasional farm, often with the broken, dilapidated remains of windmill sails protruding up into the sky against the blood-red of the sunset. Under the surface of the island there were huge underground lakes full of fresh water and the windmills had been used to draw up the water which was stored in small reservoirs at each farm and used to irrigate the surrounding fields. But now electric pumps were used instead and the once picturesque windmills were gradually falling into disrepair.

The fields on all sides were carefully planted, every available inch of the rich red-brown earth being utilised by the peasant farmers and lovingly cultivated as they had been for centuries. In the distance Kate could just make out the outline of high mountains, a darker mass against the gathering darkness of the night. There were few lights to be seen now that they had left the garish neon of the coastal hotels behind, but halfway up the hillside a cluster of pinpricks showed where a village nestled on the rocky heights.

They came to a gap in the low stone wall where a signboard said, 'Villa Margareta', and the car turned in to drive up a long, straight, and very dusty track through the fields to an irregularly shaped, one-storied building surrounded by several short, stumpy trees. She had arrived.

Kate paid off the taxi and watched its lights disappear back along the main road. The air here was very warm and seemed to wrap round her like a blanket as it had done when she stepped off the plane, but there the air had been full of the acrid smell of aeroplane fuel and jet engines, here it was sweet and clean, heavy with the scents of the flowering shrubs and climbing plants clustered round the villa. Crickets sounded loudly in the long grass and a gentle breeze rustled the leaves of the olive trees, their branches silvered in the moonlight. Kate stood there for several minutes, taking it all in, letting the peacefulness of the place enfold her, before she opened her bag and fished out the key that Simon had given her and turned to go in.

To call it a villa was rather pretentious, for the building had originally been an ordinary peasant farmhouse, and although Margie and Simon had modernised it quite a lot, no amount of work could have turned it into a glossy showplace. And luckily they hadn't tried to; they had kept the old fireplaces and stone floors and the small windows that kept the rooms cool in even the hottest weather. Instead they had concentrated on adding a very modern bathroom and kitchen and filling the place with traditional Spanish furniture and gaily coloured rugs, curtains and cushions that brightened the rooms and took off the stark whiteness of the walls.

After bringing in her suitcases, Kate carefully unpacked her clothes, her mouth twisting as she hung up the expensive, sophisticated dresses that she had bought for the honeymoon. Hurriedly she put the rest of the things away anyhow, trying not to remember, not to think. In the kitchen she found a list that Simon had written out with instructions on how to turn on the water, electricity etc., which she read by the light of a torch. It took nearly half an hour to do all these things —which had to be done in exactly the right order or else everything would seize up apparently. The idiosyncrasies of Spanish plumbing having been conquered, Kate stepped back with some satisfaction as she found that the lights worked and water came out of the taps. There were several tins of food in the kitchen larder, so she opened a tin of coffee but didn't bother with anything to eat; she was still feeling too completely miserable to care about food.

A steady, rather loud whirring noise from somewhere outside had been in the background ever since she had turned on the water and electricity and now caught her attention fully, making her wonder rather anxiously whether she'd done something wrong. Pushing open a door leading out of the kitchen, she found herself in a large walled courtyard with, in the centre of it, a moderately sized swimming pool, now empty, its glazed blue tiles gleaming in the moonlight. Past the pool, at the other end of the courtyard, there was another building, a square white tower about thirty feet high with flights of steps going up the outside. And at the top of the tower there was the cause of the noise; a twelve-sailed windmill that revolved slowly in the breeze, drawing up the water to fill the pool from the vast store deep in the core of the earth.

Hastily Kate got Simon's list of instructions again and found out how to release the water into the pool; she had alarmed visions of it blowing a gasket or something, but she merely had to turn a valve and soon the water was trickling out of a pipe to slowly cover the tiles. In a storeroom at the base of the tower she found a folding chair and brought it out to sit in the courtyard in a corner that was fragrant with the drifting scents of orange trees and hibiscus flowers while she waited for the pool to fill.

Among the stars in the velvet darkness of the sky, small moving lights appeared as a plane winged its way across the horizon, heading westward. She could imagine the passengers aboard it, going excitedly on their way; just as she should have been sitting beside Hugo that very minute, on her way to the luxury hotel in the Bahamas that he had chosen for their honeymoon.

Tears came then, tears of bitter hurt and loss, great sobs that racked her body but did nothing to ease the misery and unhappiness in her heart. She cried for a long time, huddled in the chair, until there were no tears left. And then she deliberately let herself remember.

CHAPTER TWO

THEY had met, of all places, at a charity fashion show. It had been arranged by a woman relative of Hugo's and he had been coerced into going along to give it support, which he did by donating a large sum to the charity and then standing at the back of the room sipping champagne and looking rather bored with the whole proceedings. As Kate came out on to the catwalk for the first time, dressed in a multi-shaded dress with matching jacket, her hair hidden beneath a close-fitting hat, the bright lights dazzled her momentarily and she looked over them, aware of the chattering audience but unable to see them clearly. And then a man walked from the shadows into the edge of the pool of light. She noticed that he was very tall and dark, and that he was looking up at her with an arrested expression on his face, the drink in his hand forgotten, but then it was time for her to turn and return along the catwalk to make room for the next model.

When she came out again, in a heavy woollen, rather masculine-looking outfit with high-heeled boots this time, he was still there, but there was a more speculative look on his face as he watched her. Kate had seen that look before on other men's faces and knew from bitter experience that it inevitably led to a proposition. Tossing her head, she lifted her chin high and swept past him with the swaggering walk that suited the more mannish garments. She rather thought he must have got the message, because when she next came out into the limelight, and for the rest of the show, he was gone.

Because it was a charity event the models had given their services free, so after the parade they put on their own clothes and came back to mingle with the guests. Kate accepted a glass of champagne because that was all there was on offer, and sipped it sparingly. Alcohol was too high in calories and she avoided it whenever possible. The fashion editor of one of the monthly glossies came up to her to tell her about an idea she had had to feature a range of outfits in shades of turquoise.

'With your hair you'll be ideal to show them off. Could you do it, do you think?'

'I'd like to, but it rather depends when. I'm pretty heavily booked at the moment and I'm due to go to Greece next month for a photo session on some summer fashions.'

'Well, I'll get in touch with your agency and fit it in round your commitments. I didn't think you went abroad so much now?'

'No, I don't. Luckily I'm able to pick and choose my assignments, so I'm not forever living out of a suitcase, but this offer was too interesting to turn down.'

They chatted for a little longer until one of the organisers, a grey-haired but beautifully preserved woman, came to interrupt them and the editor wandered away. The woman took Kate by the arm and slowly but insistently led her across the large, ornate room, saying, 'It was so kind of you to give your time to help our organisation. I know how busy you must be.'

Soon they had reached the far end of the room where a knot of people were gathered. One of the men there turned round as the woman spoke his name and Kate found herself looking into the grey eyes of the man who had been watching her so intently. The eyes looked into hers rather lazily and there was a slight twist of amusement on his lips when he saw her face tighten.

'Hugo, let me introduce you to our star model, Katherine Selby. Miss Selby, this is a nephew of mine, Hugo Merrion. He's something clever in the City.' And then the woman was gone, swallowed up in the laughing, casually expensive throng of people.

'Miss Selby.' He acknowledged the introduction.

Kate nodded and would have moved on, annoyed at being manipulated, but he stepped forward to bar her way.

'I thought you modelled the clothes extremely well.'

Deciding to freeze him from the outset, her eyebrows rose slightly and Kate said coldly, 'Thank you. You've been to fashion shows before, then?'

'No, I haven't, as a matter of fact.'

'Then how would you know whether I modelled them well or not?' She let her eyes run over the well-cut business suit he was wearing. 'It obviously isn't your scene at all,' she added rather disdainfully.

His lips curled into a thin smile. 'And just what is my scene?'

'A plush office with a big desk and lots of staff to whom you delegate, I expect,' she replied tartly.

To her surprise he laughed. 'You don't pull your punches, do you? When will you let me take you out to dinner so that I can show you how wrong you are?'

Kate set her glass down on a handy table before she raised her eyes to look at him and said deliberately, 'I'm sorry, Mr Merrion, but I'm not interested in finding out.' Then she turned to leave, knowing without looking back that he was standing watching her.

It was quite late that evening, when she was getting together everything she would need for the next day's assignments, that the phone rang.

'Miss Selby?' The voice on the other end was unfamiliar. 'This is Hugo Merrion. We met earlier today.'

Startled, she asked, 'How did you get my number? It's ex-directory.'

There was some amusement in his voice as he answered, 'I persuaded a friend of yours to give it to me. I was also told that you're a ballet lover.'

'So what?'

'So I have two tickets for the Ballet Rambert for next Friday. Will you come?'

'Look, Mr Merrion, I've already told you that I'm not interested. I don't go out with casual acquaintances.'

'But how can I become more than a casual acquaintance if you won't let me get to know you better?' he asked reasonably.

Annoyed because he wouldn't take no for an answer, she said shortly and untruthfully, 'I'm sorry, I'm busy on Friday.'

'Then break the date,' he suggested softly.

'No way. Goodnight, Mr Merrion.'

After that he rang her every night at the same time. At first she cut him short, but gradually the conversation lengthened as he became more persuasive until eventually, almost in exasperation, she agreed to go out with him.

She regretted the decision as soon as she'd put the phone down; there had been too many others like him during her modelling career for her not to know the pattern. Men from outside the rag trade saw these beautiful, glamorous models and got the idea that they were playgirls who would go to bed with them in return for a good time—little better than prostitutes, in fact. It was only among her own world, where everyone knew just how hard and how long the girls had to work at their assignments and on their grooming, that a man knew that when a girl said no she really meant it. There were exceptions, of course—Margie and Simon were a case in point—but Kate had fallen into the trap several times before and it had always led to the same proposition and the same recriminations when she had refused point blank. And now she'd been stupid enough to let herself be talked into yet another version of the same scene.

But this time, to avoid getting as far as a proposition, she deliberately behaved very badly. She wore a kinky, almost punk outfit, put on a wig of fair, almost white hair that stuck out in tight waves all round her head like a Millais painting, wore far too much make-up, and topped the whole thing off with lots of bracelets, earrings, and pendants with ornamental razor blades and safety pins and things on them. When she stepped back to get a complete picture of herself in the full-length mirror, she laughed aloud. The fashion mags would have raved about her, it was really way out, but she could imagine the effect it would have on the suave and elegant but very square Hugo Merrion—he wouldn't be able to ditch her fast enough.

She was supposed to meet him at the Festival Hall, but she purposefully kept him waiting for nearly half an hour. He was standing nonchalantly in the foyer, dressed in an immaculate dark blue velvet evening jacket, smoking a cigarette and seemingly quite unperturbed by the possibility that she might have stood him up. He recognised her at once, which surprised and rather annoyed her, and ground out his cigarette to come forward to take her hand.

'Hallo. Glad you could make it.' He helped her with her cloak and didn't even blink at the sight of the kinky gear. 'Shall we go in straightaway? I think the performance is about to start.'

Which was a polite way of saying that they were already very late. But when they were shown to their seats Kate found that he had booked a box for the two of them and there were chocolates and a bottle of very expensive perfume already waiting there for her. He certainly did things in style, she admitted, but didn't think any more of him for going to such lengths to impress her.

In the interval she turned to him and said, 'A box to ourselves—how extravagant!'

He smiled lazily. 'I like to watch the ballet in comfort, and when you're as tall as I am sitting in the stalls with your knees tucked up round your neck is no fun, believe me, but here I can stretch out.'

'Oh, I see. I hadn't thought of that.'

'No, I thought you might not have,' he replied equably, then stood up and suggested they go to the bar for a drink.

He raised his brows a little when she asked for a fruit juice. 'I suppose you have to watch your figure?'

'It *is* my fortune,' she replied shortly.

Casually he said, 'Then you must already be a millionairess.'

Kate looked at him quickly but could read nothing

in his face; he was merely looking at her with a slightly enigmatic smile. And if it was intended as a compliment, it was the nearest he got to one all evening. She thought he would have taken her on to somewhere where he wasn't known, but after the ballet he took her to Quaglinos where they ate and talked about ballet mostly and other, equally impersonal, topics. Several people he knew greeted him and were obviously curious about Kate, and he even introduced her to one or two of them, which she thought was pretty remarkable when she looked so like a weirdo. They watched the cabaret and afterwards he asked her to dance. He didn't try to kiss her or paw her, holding her loosely and letting her go again at once if he had to pull her close to avoid a collision. Kate looked at him with a little frown of puzzlement between her brows; he was different from what she had anticipated, but not so different that she didn't expect him to proposition her some time during the evening.

It was late when he drew up outside her flat and turned off the engine. Here it comes, she thought; he'll say, 'Aren't you going to ask me in for a nightcap?' and as soon as he gets in my flat he'll start the Casanova bit. Silently she waited.

Hugo came round and opened the door for her. 'Can you manage alone or would you like me to see you to your door?'

Kate's eyes widened in surprise as she got out. 'I can manage, thanks.'

'Then I'll wish you goodnight. When may I see you again?'

'You—you want to?'

'Oh, yes, I want to.'

Her mind in a whirl, Kate found herself agreeing to go out with him again the following day.

He came to call for her, as elegant as ever, and this time she had dressed normally, her shining hair falling in soft curls around her face, her dress a sophisticated yet simple swathed sheaf that enhanced her tall, slim figure.

Hugo ran his eyes over her appreciatively. 'I see that I'm forgiven.'

'Forgiven?'

'Yes. Wasn't that what you were doing last night? Punishing me for coercing you into making a date with me against your will?'

Kate gulped; this man knew far too much about the workings of the female mind for her liking. He must have had dozens of girl-friends to be that experienced, she realised. Looking at him rather doubtfully, she began to wonder just what she was getting into, but he gave her no time to dwell on it, picking up her stole to put it round her shoulders and saying, 'Shall we go?' before whisking her away to the theatre in his Jaguar.

That was how it had started, and from then on they saw each other almost every day, if not in the evening then for lunch or a cocktail. Everywhere they went he made sure that they had the best seats, the best food and drink; he spent generously but not ostentatiously, taking her to concerts and art galleries as well as night-clubs and restaurants. Kate found him witty and enter-taining, ready to talk on any subject that interested her —and he didn't talk down to her as if she was an empty-headed doll as some of the other men she'd dated had. She found out that 'something clever in the City' meant that he was a director of a merchant bank that had been in his family for generations, and was also on the boards of several other commercial companies, his position being mostly inherited from his father who had retired a few years ago. He was also interested in sport and played squash several times a week, which accounted for his athletic fitness, Kate decided after he took her to watch him playing an extremely fast and furious match.

She was at first surprised and then gradually more intrigued by the fact that he didn't make a pass at her, never paying her fulsome compliments or trying to touch her. And slowly she began to feel somewhat piqued by the fact, wondering just why he was taking her out so much when he didn't even try to kiss her. He knew far too much about women for him not to have had affairs in the past, so why?

It was on the eve of her departure to Greece, when they had been going together for nearly four weeks, and they were walking through the gardens surrounding a riverside nightclub beneath a crisp March moon, that he suddenly stopped and said, 'Oh, yes, there was something I meant to do.' And he drew her gently into his arms and kissed her.

As a first kiss it was really something. It left Kate clinging to him weakly as he said rather unsteadily, 'I must remember to do that again some time.' He grinned at the look on her face and laughingly ran her along to the car-park to drive her home in his new silver Jaguar.

She was away for nearly two weeks, a busy, hectic time when she had to work during every hour of daylight and was too tired to do anything but sleep the rest of the time. Flying back with the rest of the photographic team, they arrived at Heathrow airport about eight-thirty in the evening and Hugo was waiting for her, his height and bearing setting him apart from the crowd. There was something about him—panache was the only word she could find to describe it. At the sight of him, Kate felt her heart give a mad, dizzying lurch and she knew then, suddenly, that she had fallen for him.

He stepped forward to meet her and she found herself hurrying towards him, trying not to let her eyes give her away but unable to prevent herself gazing up at him in wonderment. Could she really have fallen for this man whom she still felt that she didn't really know, who always seemed to hold back some part of himself that she was never allowed to see? As he bent to kiss her lightly on the forehead, she knew with utmost certainty that for the first time in her life she was head over heels in love.

During the next few minutes, when she was saying goodbye to the rest of the team and Hugo was finding a luggage trolley for her cases, she was able to recover her composure a little and smile and talk animatedly to him about her trip while they walked to his waiting car. After stowing her cases in the boot, he drove her to a small, intimate restaurant where the lighting was subdued and the food and service excellent.

'You always seem to find marvellous places to eat,' Kate remarked with a smile as she sat back after finishing a delicious lemon soufflé.

'I try to make a point of never settling for second best.'

'Not in anything?' she asked lightly.

'Not in anything,' he replied with a firmness that

startled her a little. She looked at him searchingly but could read nothing in his expression, and for the hundredth time wished that she could fathom out what made him tick, what lay behind the cool, enigmatic façade he presented to the world. That there was another side, she was sure, but he had never let her see it; he had never shown anger, hate, jealousy—even when he'd kissed her he hadn't lost control of his emotions.

He looked up and caught her watching him, his mouth twisting into a faintly sardonic curl, but he merely said, 'Would you like another coffee?' And when she shook her head, 'Shall we go, then?'

When they got to her flat he carried her cases up for her and for the first time she invited him to stay and have a drink. He accepted and they sat companionably together on the settee and talked, but Kate felt nervous and on edge; not because she was afraid of him, but because of this new and very wonderful feeling that filled her heart. She didn't want to sit here talking just as if the most momentous thing in her life had never happened, she wanted to dance and sing with happiness, and most of all she wanted to tell Hugo that she loved him. But she couldn't do that, not yet. Not until he showed that he felt the same way. But she had no idea how he really felt about her; she couldn't tell whether he just liked her company, whether he took her out because she was a beautiful adornment that made other men envy him, or if he had some genuine feelings for her. Her hand trembling, Kate lifted her glass to drink, letting her hair fall forward to hide her face.

Hugo's hand reached out and took the glass from her, setting it down on the table, then came back to take her hand firmly in his. 'You're shaking. I'm sorry, I didn't realise how tired you were. I'll push off and let you get some sleep.' He stood up and pulled her up beside him. 'You're not working tomorrow, are you?'

'No, thank goodness. I haven't any assignments until Wednesday.'

'Good. Then you can sleep late in the morning. May I see you tomorrow night? There's a new opera at Covent Garden, would you like to see it?'

He was still holding her loosely by the arms and she let her hands move slowly up his lapels. 'Yes, but— would you mind if we went dancing instead?'

His eyebrows rose slightly. 'Not if you'd prefer it. Till tomorrow, then. Goodnight, sweet Kate. Sleep well.' He kissed her lightly on the forehead again and turned to go.

Kate found that she didn't want him to go like this, with just a casual goodbye, not tonight of all nights. She lifted her hand towards him. 'Hugo.'

'Yes?'

Slowly she dropped her hand and shook her head. 'Oh—nothing.'

'Just—Hugo?'

'Yes.' Her glance met his and she thought she saw an understanding light in his eyes—understanding and something else she couldn't fathom.

He stepped forward, pulled her to him, and kissed her hard on the mouth. Then he straightened, gave her his usual lazy smile, and was gone, leaving her with the room still spinning about her head.

The following day Kate took pains with her make-up and clothes, putting on a softly clinging dress that she had bought in Greece in a deep, deep red colour that emphasised the slender lines of her figure. Her hair she put up in a sophisticated, off-the-face style; somehow she always felt that she needed to look very sophisticated when she was with Hugo, not just because he was ten years older, but because he was always so completely self-possessed that to keep up with him she had to appear to be like that too, even if inside she knew herself to be young and unworldly in comparison.

He called for her promptly at eight and took her to a new nightclub that had recently been opened by a rather notorious playboy, where the way-out decor was mercifully shrouded by the dim lighting, but where the food was good and there were lots of celebrities among the patrons for the rubberneckers to stare at. But Kate wasn't interested in anyone but Hugo. She had an overwhelming feeling of excitement inside her that seemed to heighten all her senses, bringing a vital, sparkling glow to her eyes and making her intensely aware of everything around her, as if she must take in every sensation and hold it fast, remember it forever. Intoxicating tremors of exhilaration ran through her whenever he touched her, however casually, and when he drew her close to him when they danced, his eyes smiling into hers, she felt as if her heart would burst with happiness, and for Kate they might have been alone together, so oblivious was she of everyone else in the place. There was just the two of them, so close and yet so far apart, and the dreamy, insistent beat of the music.

Perhaps Hugo, too, shared her feelings, for it was still quite early when he suggested they leave. At the door of her flat he took the key from her unsteady hand and closed the door softly after them, then he unbuttoned her evening cloak, letting it fall to the floor, while his hand came up to caress the long, graceful line of her neck, his eyes very dark as they stared into hers.

Kate didn't know whether she moved forward or whether he pulled her to him, but the next second she was in his arms and this time he was kissing her with a deep, bruising hunger that left her limp and shaking when he finally lifted his head.

She could feel his heart beating loudly as she leaned her head against his shoulder and he said thickly, 'I want you, Kate, I've wanted you from the first moment I saw you. You're so lovely, so desirable.'

He stooped to pick her up, and Kate put her arms round his neck, letting him kiss her as he carried her along. It wasn't until he laid her down and she realised that she was lying on her bed that she came to her senses with a sickening jolt.

Hurriedly she sat up, pushing him away from her. 'Hugo, please!'

She tried to roll off the bed, but he caught her and pulled her back, pressing her down on to the pillows as he tried to kiss her again, his eyes dark with a desire he didn't attempt to hide now. Quickly she turned her face away and lay quite still. After a moment he sat back and released her hands.

'What's the matter?' he asked unevenly.

'Hugo, I don't want this.'

She looked up at him pleadingly, wanting him to understand, but his eyes narrowed and he said sharply, 'That isn't true! Tonight you wanted it as much as I do. It may have been for the first time, but you wanted me all right.'

'No, not—like this.'

He stared down at her for a moment, his lips a thin, hard line in his face. Then he raised a hand to push back his hair and stood up. 'I beg your pardon. I see we should have got the preliminaries over first. Shall we go back into the sitting-room and discuss your—terms?'

Turning abruptly, he walked out of the bedroom while Kate followed him more slowly, his choice of words creating a fear that made her heart sink within her. When she walked into the room he was standing by the window, smoking a cigarette and gazing out.

'Do you think I could have a drink?'

'Of—of course. Help yourself.'

'Thanks.' He crossed to the wall unit and poured a whisky from the decanter, then went to sit in an armchair, looking at her while he sipped the drink. Tersely he said, 'Perhaps I should have made myself plain at the outset. But I thought you were the romantic type— which just shows you how wrong you can be,' he added caustically. 'Don't worry, Kate, I fully intended to pay for my pleasures. I haven't—courted you for the past month just for a casual affair. I'll provide you with a flat, or take over the rent of this one, if you'd prefer it, and I'll pay all your bills and expenses so long as you're my mistress.'

Kate leant back against the wall, feeling suddenly sick and empty inside. 'Your—mistress?'

'An old-fashioned word, I admit, but one that adequately sums up the situation, I think.'

Her mind reeling as if he had hit her, Kate was aware only of the need to hide her feelings from him, not to let him see how much he had hurt her. Her pride at least she would try to keep intact even if her heart and mind were shattered into fragments. Somehow she forced herself to walk across the room and stand with her back to him while she poured herself a drink. 'You're very—generous,' she managed.

'I hope that you will be too,' he replied silkily.

With her fingers gripping the glass tightly she was able to control her voice enough to say, 'And when you grow tired of me?'

'You're far too lovely for that to happen for quite some time, but if it does ...' he shrugged, 'then I shall make sure that you receive adequate financial compensation.'

Anger came to her then, and with it a deep bitterness that he should think her immoral enough to accept his offer. She turned to face him as he lounged casually in the chair. 'A sort of redundancy payment, you mean?'

He was quite unperturbed. 'Call it more of a golden handshake.' He set down his glass and rose. 'Well, do you accept my offer?' When she didn't answer he crossed to stand close to her. 'I thought you would prefer it if we went to bed together before we discussed this. You won't be disappointed, Kate, I promise you,' he added softly.

Kate stared at him for a moment before turning and walking a few steps away from him. Then she squared her shoulders and faced him again. 'Are you a man of principle, Hugo?'

His brows rose at the unexpectedness of the question. 'I hope so.'

'Well, I happen to live by principles too. Perhaps rather old-fashioned ones in this day and age, but I intend to keep them all the same. So thanks, but the answer's no.'

He frowned. 'What's the matter? Isn't my offer high enough for you? Or do you have another fat fish dangling on the hook?' he asked sarcastically.

Kate flushed angrily, but tried to keep her temper. 'There's really no point in discussing this any further. I'm not going to change my mind, Hugo.'

'Everyone has a price.'

'Do they?'

'Oh, yes.' He came to cup her face in his hand, forcing her chin up so that she had to look at him. 'So won't you name yours? I'm a reasonable man, Kate, and I'll meet your demands if I can. Because I want to go to bed with you very much, and I rather think you want it, too, despite what you've said.'

'Do I?'

'You gave me enough encouragement tonight to think so.' And he lowered his head to kiss her gently, lingeringly on the mouth. 'So what is it, Kate?'

She shook her head, not looking at him. 'You wouldn't even begin to understand. Maybe you were right, maybe I am the romantic type. I'm certainly not the kind of girl you think me, and I don't want a cold-blooded sexual relationship.'

Hugo gave a crooked grin. 'There won't be anything cold-blooded about it, I assure you.'

Kate bit her lip, then said coldly, 'I think you'd better leave.'

His jaw tightened and he frowned, showing anger for the first time. 'My God, you must think I'm green! I don't know what your game is, but I'm willing to bet that you've slept with any number of men, not to mention using your body to further your career. If you're trying to blow hot and then cold for some reason, why don't you come right out and say it? I've told you already that I'll....'

He broke off abruptly as Kate faced him, her eyes blazingly angry in her chalk-white face. 'How dare you insult me like that? Get out of my home! Go on, get the hell out of here!'

His eyes widened incredulously. 'Good God, I really believe you mean it!'

'I mean it all right. If you don't get out of here I'll call the police and have you thrown out!' Tears of fury came into her eyes and she made a wild plunge towards the phone, but before she could reach it he caught her by the wrists and pulled her round to face him, still staring at her disbelievingly.

'If you're so straight-laced why did you let me come up here and kiss you like I did? Why didn't you stop me?'

Kate stood trembling in his grip, willing herself not to cry in front of him. Angrily she blinked back the tears. 'Because you'd never made a pass at me before. Because I thought I could trust you.'

'How could you possibly be so naïve? Be your age, Kate, this is the twentieth century, not the eighteenth. Do you really expect me to believe that you're going to wait around for some knight in shining armour to come along and sweep you off your feet? You must have known that I....' He stopped abruptly, then said slowly, 'You surely didn't think that I....'

Jerking herself free of him, she interrupted him quickly before he could go on, before he guessed the truth. 'Why don't you just go away and leave me alone? You live your life the way you want to and I'll live mine.' She ran across to the front door and opened it, waiting until he came slowly across to her.

'Kate....'

'Goodbye, Hugo.' She remained standing there, taut-faced, until he gave a little shrug, turned on his heel and she was at last able to slam the door behind him and run to throw herself on her bed in a storm of weeping.

So it had lasted just a day. To fall in love for the very first time and then to have it thrown back in your face within twenty-four hours must be some kind of record, she told herself cynically as she looked in the mirror the next day and regarded the ravages that crying for hours had done to her face. Cynicism was new to her nature, something she had never had to resort to before, but it stopped her from crying, and crying was definitely bad for business when the all-seeing lens of a camera was pointing at you all day long. By using far more make-up than she normally would, she managed to cover up the worst of the damage and arrived at her first assignment on time. This was a photo-fashion session at Hampstead Heath fair, but now the amusements were still and the sideshows devoid of life, a ghostlike place that echoed the unhappiness she felt, but where she had to pose and smile, smile, smile, just as if she hadn't a care in the world.

It was the first job in a busy schedule, but in a strange way she found that work helped, that it stopped her from thinking of Hugo, and she even phoned her agent to take on more assignments for the days she normally kept free. She didn't want to have time to think, but she still lay awake at night, miserably wishing that things could have worked out differently. It couldn't last, of course; one day she felt faint while modelling and the designer gave her a good talking to and sent for her agent. He scratched his head a bit, took her out for a meal and then made her go home and go to bed. She slept, on and off, for nearly twenty-four hours and then felt better, still far from happy, but able to cope with life again and more determined than ever not to let herself fall for a man until she was absolutely sure of him, trying to put the whole thing behind her and count it as just one of those debit side experiences.

One evening, almost a month after she'd split with Hugo, Kate threw a party at her flat to celebrate the birthday of one of her friends. It was an informal affair where everyone knew each other and drink and flashbulbs were consumed at an equal rate. The atmosphere was friendly, if rather noisy, and Kate was kept busy changing records, passing round food and generally doing her duty as hostess. At about eleven she heard the doorbell ring above the music and went to answer it, expecting to welcome some latecomer.

When she opened the door the smile on her face swiftly gave way to amazement. Hugo was standing in the doorway in a dinner jacket, the collar turned up and the shoulders wet with rain. Kate found that she couldn't speak, could only stare at him like an idiot.

He looked searchingly at her face, then glanced past her at the crowded room. 'I'm afraid I called at a bad time.'

'Yes,' she managed.

Surprisingly he seemed somewhat at a loss. 'I—I

wanted to talk to you. I suppose I should have phoned first—but I was afraid you'd slam the receiver down on me.'

'Afraid?' She looked at him disbelievingly.

'Yes.'

Then the hurt started to come back and she said shortly, 'You're right, I would have done.'

He stepped swiftly into the room and said urgently, 'Kate, I have to talk to you. Isn't there somewhere quiet where we could go?'

For a moment longer she continued to gaze at him, then she shrugged. 'You'd better come into the kitchen.' She shut the front door and led the way through the gyrating dancers, squeezed past a couple of graphic artists who were talking shop, and into the kitchen, shutting out the noise as she shut the door behind them.

'Would you like a drink?' Kate turned her back on him and walked over to the table, pretending to busy herself by stacking plates, but all the time wishing that her heart would stop pounding and wondering why he'd come, why he had even dared to show his face here again. If he'd come to renew his sordid offer, if he had —her fingers tightened round the neck of a bottle— she'd smash him over the head with it!

'Thank you, no. Kate I....' He paused. 'Kate, please look at me.'

Slowly she turned to face him, her hands behind her gripping the table, her face set and cold. 'Well?'

'I haven't stopped thinking about you since the last time I saw you,' he said slowly. 'I know I made the most colossal blunder then and I haven't stopped regretting it since. I know that I hurt you and I'm sorry for it. It would make me very happy if you'd forgive me, Kate, and even happier if you'd let me start again from the beginning.'

'Why? So that it could have the same ending?' she asked bitterly. 'I haven't changed, Hugo. My answer would still be the same.'

'But I won't make the mistake of asking the same question,' he said quickly. 'Forgive me, Kate. Forgive me and say you'll start again.'

'Just like that? You walk in here and say you're sorry and expect me to smile and say, "That's all right, Hugo, just one of those things!" Well, it isn't as easy as that!' She turned hurriedly away from him and walked across the kitchen. Hugo took a step towards her, but just then the door opened and a laughing, singing couple came in.

'Katie love, we've run out of ice,' the man told her.

'Oh, there's some in the top of the fridge.'

He went to get some, oblivious of the taut atmosphere in the room, but the girl was more sensitive, looking quickly at Kate's set face and Hugo's frown. When her escort seemed as if he wanted to stay and chat, she pulled him firmly out of the door.

When they'd gone they still stood at opposite ends of the room, a little pool of silence between them. Then Hugo said heavily, 'I know that I was every kind of a fool that night, but I just couldn't believe. . . .' He broke off and came to stand in front of her, his hands in his pockets, his hair still damp from the rain, 'I've been cursing myself ever since, wanting to come back, but sure that you'd have nothing more to do with me. Tonight I couldn't stand it any longer. I walked around for hours and kept finding myself on your doorstep. So here I am.' His eyes scanned her face, looking for some sign of what she was thinking, but she was looking down, her expression unreadable. At length he said simply, 'I missed you, Kate.'

Slowly she raised her eyes and found him watching her intently. For a moment she continued to gaze at him, then she gave a little choking sob. 'Oh, Hugo, you fool! You big fool!' And the next instant she was held tightly in his arms and being hugged so hard that she thought her ribs would crack.

When Hugo took her out again for the first time, Kate naturally felt rather tense and strained, wondering how things could ever be the same between them. She had forgiven him after very little persuasion or apology on his part, she knew, but she was so crazy about him that she had been more than happy to meet him halfway. But now Hugo's manner towards her had changed. The differences were subtle but definitely there; the way he looked at her as if she was special, treating her as something fragile that might break, taking her to society parties and introducing her to a different set of friends.

And one late April weekend, when the pink cherry blossom was bursting into flower and the drifting daffodils were raising their heads to the spring sunshine, he drove her deep into the countryside to stay at his parents' home. Any diffidence she might have felt was soon dispelled by the warm welcome they gave her and she quickly felt at ease as they showed her round the lovely old Tudor manor house with its mellow brickwork, latticed windows, and tall, ornate chimneys.

On the afternoon of their second day there, Hugo took her for a walk to the ruins of a nearby castle and here he took a ring from his pocket and slipped it on to the third finger of her left hand.

'This is a betrothal ring that the eldest son of my family traditionally gives to the girl he wants to marry.' He still held her hand and his eyes studied her face searchingly. 'Will you wear it for me, Kate? Will you?'

Kate found that she was too choked up to speak and had to raise a finger to wipe sudden tears from her cheeks. She looked at his face, her eyes full of love and happiness. Then she walked into the circle of his arms and clung to him unashamedly.

Hugo reached down to lift her face from where it was buried in his shoulder and tilted her chin to look at her. 'I take it that means yes?' he asked softly.

'Oh, yes! Oh, Hugo, I love you so very much,' she confessed at last.

And then his lips were on hers with the same yearning hunger that he had shown before, when he had made a very different proposal. But now everything was changed and the longed-for dream had become reality.

'Darling, we'll get married very soon. There's nothing to wait for and I want so much to claim you as my bride. We shall be married in June.'

We shall be married in June. The words echoed hollowly in Kate's head as she sat in the courtyard of the old windmill, alone in the darkness. She shivered, the night had turned cold now. She held her arms and rubbed them. The pool was full, too full really, the water lapping gently almost at the brim. She rose and switched off the pump, looked again up at the sky, then turned and went slowly into the house.

CHAPTER THREE

A loud discordant ringing noise woke her the next morning and for a few moments Kate couldn't think where she was. It sounded as if a coachload of campanologists had been let loose outside the house, and she hastily jumped out of bed and pushed the shutters wide to find out the cause of the din. In the field next to the house a very small boy under a very large straw hat was driving a herd of about fifty scrawny-looking sheep into a field further along. Each of the sheep had a metal bell round its neck, which accounted for all the noise. They threw up clouds of dust as they ran over the parched fields, encouraged by shouts from the boy who prodded them along with a stick. Presumably the sheep were just as eager to get to new pasture, but what grass there was in the new field was already short and stubbly, which probably accounted for the thin, bony appearance of the poor creatures.

Closing her eyes, Kate threw her head back and breathed in the smell of the grass and trees and clean air, delicious, and the weather was perfect too; sparkling, golden sunshine that was already as warm as a caress. For a while she stood at the window taking in all the scenery that had just been dark shapes against the moonlit sky last night. She could just make out the road, about a hundred yards away, at the end of the long, straight driveway. Between it and the house on one side there were rows and rows of gnarled olive trees, their trunks twisted and misshapen like the arthritic fingers of an old, old woman. On the other side of the driveway the sheep fields reached to another farmhouse, almost identical with the villa, but there the sails of the windmill had been let fall into the usual state of disrepair, the farmer presumably preferring to use more modern methods of irrigation. Kate could see people already at work there: a buxom woman in a green dress who hung washing out on a line, a short, thin man in the inevitable straw hat who was hoeing in a field of vegetables, and a boy even younger than the shepherd who was collecting eggs from under hens who were so free that they seemed to range all over the yard and the farm too.

Eggs. The thought of them made Kate realise how hungry she was. Perhaps the farmer would sell her some. Quickly she showered and put on slacks and a sun-top, adding dark glasses to hide the puffiness round her eyes caused by crying herself to sleep last night, and trying determinedly, but not very successfully, not to let herself think of Hugo and the future, to concentrate on the present and live from hour to hour. After some searching she found a basket of Margie's in a cupboard and set off down the driveway. It would have been quicker to hop over the stone walls and go across the fields, but Kate didn't want to risk offending the farmer so took the long way round, practising asking for eggs in Spanish as she went. During her years as a model she had visited Spanish-speaking countries several times so had picked up a smattering of the language. She had even been to Majorca a couple of years earlier on an assignment, but then she had stayed at a hotel in Palma, the capital, and her only excursions had been to the mile upon mile of golden beaches along the narrow strips of coast on either side of Palma, where hundreds of hotels, bars and restaurants spread along the shoreline like garish pieces of costume jewellery.

The child saw her coming first and ran to fetch the farmer's wife, who looked her up and down curiously but greeted her with a polite, *'Buenos dias, señorita.'*

They had a halting conversation, the Majorcan accent being to pure Spanish what the Scotch accent is to English, but Kate managed to buy eggs and some home-made bread and cheese. Luckily she had been able to change some money at the airport the day before and so was able to pay for them in pesetas. The elder boy and the farmer came along to see what it was all about and the farmer gave her some tomatoes out of their own garden, for which he refused payment. By much waving of the arms they made it understood that she was welcome to call there for supplies any day, so they parted with smiles and polite bobbing bows. The two boys, Miguel and Pepito, insisted on escorting her back to the villa; they were avidly curious about the house but were too shy to ask to see it, so Kate took them in and showed them round. They exclaimed with wonder and excitement at all the modern gadgets, especially the pool, and jabbered away to each other, obviously storing everything up to tell their parents.

After they had gone, Kate changed into a bikini and ate a leisurely breakfast at the side of the pool. There was a bookcase stuffed with paperbacks in the living-room and she chose one and settled in a lounger to read while she sunbathed, but after a little while she threw the book aside, unable to concentrate, her mind forever slipping away from the story as she wondered

what Hugo was doing now; whether he was trying to
find her, whether Simon had written to him as he had
promised and what Hugo would do when he got the
letter. That he would go to see Simon to try to find out
where she was, she was pretty sure, but she knew that
Simon could be trusted not to give her whereabouts
away. Worriedly she tried to guess how long it would
take for the annulment to go through, and whether she
would have to appear in court and give evidence or
something. She had only the vaguest idea about the
procedure, but imagined it must be similar to a divorce.
Fervently she hoped that she wouldn't have to state
her reasons for running away; to have to stand up and
tell the world that Hugo neither loved her nor trusted
her, that he had married her only to possess her, would
be more than she could bear.

Raising her hands to her head, Kate pressed her
palms hard against her temples, trying to shut out the
hateful, harrowing pictures her wayward imagination
had conjured up. But it was no good, they kept coming
back again and again, until in desperation she plunged
into the pool, swimming up and down till she was too
spent to carry on and climbed out to flop down in the
sun, too tired to even think. Later that day she could
only be bothered to eat the rest of the bread and
cheese, but the following morning she roused herself
enough after another sleepless night to go out and buy
some more groceries. The nearest town was some miles
away, so she had to get out Simon's car from the
garage. This proved to be a little Seat, the Spanish
equivalent of a Mini, and she found it terribly awk-
ward at first, because not only was the steering wheel
on the wrong side but she had to change gear with her

right hand instead of her left. Luckily there was very
little traffic on the roads so that she was able to practise
driving on the right before she came to a busier road
through a village. The hardest part, she found, was the
roundabouts; it was positively unnerving driving the
wrong way round these and she was thankful when she
found a place to park on the outskirts of the nearest
town and relax for a minute, wiping her hands, which
had been gripping the wheel tightly, on her handkerchief.

It was market day in the town and the main square
and several side streets were thronged with shoppers
who crowded round the stalls offering fruit and vegetables, olives in all stages from fresh to pickled, as well
as fish and meat. There were also quite a few stalls
piled with merchandise to tempt the holidaymakers:
olivewood ornaments, leather goods like handbags and
thick belts with heavy brass buckles in all sorts of
designs, slippers made from goatskin, cheap pottery
and china, watches and imitation jewellery. The stalls
were interesting at first but eventually became repeti-
tive. It was still early in the season and this was an inland town, but already there were quite a few tourists
about, having come by hired car or for brief coach
stops to visit the market on their way to the more
popular tourist attractions. They stood out easily from
the native Majorcans, not only because of differences
in height and colouring, but also through their gayer,
more casual clothes, many of them dressed as Kate was,
in shorts and sun-tops.

Wandering round the food stalls, she bought enough
fruit and vegetables to last her a couple of days, taking
her time, in no hurry to go back to the villa to be

alone with her unhappy thoughts again. While she was waiting to be served with some pale yellow, rather misshapen oranges grown on the island, she felt someone watching her and looked up quickly to find a man studying her intently. He was standing only a few feet away at the other end of the stall and had the dark hair and olive complexion of a typical Spaniard, but he was better dressed than most of the men there, having on a lightweight grey suit and a white shirt and tie, which made him seem out of place in the busy market. When he saw that she had noticed him he smiled and gave a slight nod. Kate ignored him. One of the great disadvantages of having her looks was that men were always staring at her—all men, of whatever age and nationality. She had got used to it long ago, although that didn't mean that she liked it, but it was one of those things you had to come to terms with if you wanted to live with any sort of peace of mind. She accepted it and ignored it in so far as she could, just as she tried to ignore the far more hurtful looks of pure hate and malevolent jealousy she received from some women when they saw her for the first time. It was an instinctive reaction, she knew, but she could no more help being born the way she was than they could; fate—or rather her parents' genes—had given her beauty, but had more than got its own back in other ways. Like now, for instance, she thought wryly as she turned her back on the man to walk along the road to a small supermarket to get the other things she needed.

It was cooler and darker inside the shop, so she took off her large-lensed sun-specs and perched them on top of her head while she wandered round the shelves trying to find what she wanted. When she emerged from

the shop the man was standing just outside. She recognised him despite the camera he was pointing in her
direction, ready to shoot. She heard the shutter click
and glared at him indignantly, but he calmly took
another shot before grinning again and then melting
into the crowd. Kate shrugged philosophically; to take
photographs was harmless enough, and at least he
hadn't tried to talk to her. Which was fortunate for
him, because she was in no mood to politely brush off
anyone who made a pass at her right now.

Completing the rest of her shopping, Kate started to
walk back to the car, but paused when she saw a shop
selling English language magazines; perhaps they
would hold her attention more than a book. She
bought several magazines and then a copy of one of
yesterday's national dailies, which cost such an exorbi-
tant sum of pesetas that she decided a daily paper was
one extravagance she would have to do without while
she was here.

Back at the villa, she had a swim in the pool and
then cooked herself a meal, reading the paper as she
ate—a habit one acquires when living alone as she had
done on the lengthy and frequent periods when her
half-brother had been abroad. There were the usual
war, crime and political reports, but as she idly turned
the page she almost choked on her food, coughing and
having to take a drink, for there on the gossip page was
a photograph of Hugo and herself leaving the church.
She took one look at their faces and then didn't look
again; that had been another world, another era. Of
course, she should have realised that her running away
would be picked up by the more sensation-seeking
papers; it would be one of the juiciest titbits of scandal

for months. Slowly, distastefully, she began to read the story under the photograph, then read faster in growing disbelief. There was nothing, not one word, about her having walked out on Hugo! The item gave details—mostly incorrect—about her and Hugo, named the most prominent of the guests and who was supposed to be having an affair with whom, and ended by stating that the bridal pair had slipped quietly away from the reception to go to their honeymoon destination somewhere in the West Indies.

So that was how he'd covered the thing up, by getting someone—Adam Ralston, probably—to announce that they'd left without saying goodbye to avoid all the fuss. Neat! But just how long could he do a Watergate when he was due to return from honeymoon and was minus one quite important accessory—namely the bride! Kate smiled mirthlessly; Hugo might have avoided a scandal for the present, but there was no way he would be able to keep the whole thing out of the papers indefinitely.

That evening she sat down and wrote a long letter to Simon and Margie, asking lots of questions she hadn't been able to think of so soon after bolting from the wedding, like how soon would it be safe for her to return to England, could Simon get a promise from Hugo that he wouldn't come near her, and, most important of all, how soon would she be free of him forever. She also asked after her tiny godsons and told them that all was well with their villa, ending by begging them to write quickly and let her know the latest position.

The following morning she decided to walk to the nearest village to post the letter; she had toyed with the idea of driving into the town again but rejected the idea in favour of some exercise. She hadn't travelled

in the direction of the village before and found that
the way led between the usual stone walls with fields of
crops and orchards of olive and almond trees for over a
mile before it rounded a bend and the road became almost a bridge, a solid parapet with just a few yards of
scrubland on either side of the road and then the sheer
drop down into a white-walled quarry on both sides.
For a while Kate stopped to watch a machine which
moved along rails, slowly cutting its way ever deeper
into the cold white stone. A little further on the way
began to descend into a valley where the village nestled
surrounded by orange and lemon groves. The houses
were of sun-baked stone the colour of earth, their roofs
of deep-red pantiles, and their shutters were closed
against the sun behind delicate wrought-iron balconies.

Kate crossed a bridge over a steep-sided but now
completely dried-up river bed, and walked down
through the sunlit streets looking for a post office. At
first it seemed as if there were no shops at all in the
place, but then a black-clad woman pushed aside a
beaded curtain in a doorway and Kate realised that
behind it was the local butcher's shop, although there
was no sign outside to indicate the fact. After that she
found one or two other shops and eventually came
across one that did have a small sign 'Estanco', and she
knew that in this state-run tobacco shop she would be
able to buy a stamp. But knowing that there were
stamps to buy and asking for an airmail one to England
was another matter. By the time she finally made herself understood with the help of much miming, she
was beginning to think it would have been easier to
drive to Palma airport, find a crew member off one of
the many British planes that landed daily, and ask

them to take the letter back and post it for her.

The sun was high and hot when she set out to walk
back to the villa and the tarmacked road soon made her
feet ache. A tanker lorry with its red flag flying, indi-
cating that it carried a volatile material, passed her as
she plodded along. The driver tooted at her and he
and his mate waved and gave big grins as they went
towards the village. Kate rested for a while at the
quarry; the machine was still slowly slicing through
the stone amidst clouds of white dust, the screech of its
cutting saw raucous in the still air. When it reached the
end of the rails a man came and moved it back, then
lowered it to start again.

Setting off again, Kate came to a gap in the wall and
walked along in the fields under the shade of the olive
trees to avoid some of the heat. She wished she'd
thought to put on a hat—trust mad dogs and English
girls to go out in the noonday sun! she thought wryly.
From where she walked she could see that the road
swept round in a deep bend and that by cutting across
the fields she could save herself quite a walk, so she
headed away from the road, further into the fields.
Coming to another wall she looked for a gateway but
couldn't find one, so climbed nimbly over it just where
a harrow had been left close up to its shadow, the
wicked-looking spikes of the instrument almost reaching the top of the wall.

This was a more open field now, its crop of corn recently harvested and leaving only the short, dried-up
stubble, but even though there wasn't any shade, Kate
still cut across the edge of it, only too happy to shorten
the distance home. From her right she became aware of
a pounding noise and turned to see two riders galloping

across the fields in her general direction. As they jumped the wall into the field beyond hers, she saw that one was a man who was sat straight in the saddle of a big black horse, and the other a girl, quite young by the look of it, who rode a much smaller horse, hardly bigger than a pony. They came flying over the empty field, the girl well in the lead, pushing her mount for all she was worth, her face full of excitement.

Smiling, Kate watched them, enjoying secondhand the pleasure they must be deriving from the headlong gallop, then her face changed as she realised with mounting horror that they intended to jump the wall she had just climbed over—and the girl was headed straight for the section where the harrow lay hidden from view on the other side! Without stopping to think, she dropped her basket and began to run towards them, shouting frantically and waving her arms.

'Stop! Look out. It's dangerous!' Oh hell, what was the Spanish for stop? *Cuidado!* she yelled.

The man, who was further away, saw her first and began to rein in his horse, but the girl came speeding on, her whole being concentrated on the jump she was about to make. Desperately Kate ran towards her, the vision of an appalling accident already before her eyes and lending strength to her legs.

'Hi! Stop!' She continued to shout and now the man had added his voice to her own and at last they penetrated to the girl and she looked up. But it was too late, the animal was already gathering itself for the jump. With a little cry of despair, Kate threw herself across the last few feet of ground and lunged upwards to catch the horse's bridle, pulling its head down and round as hard as she could.

There was a terrible confusion of sound and movement that seemed to go on for ages but could only have lasted a few seconds. There was a scream, but whether it came from the girl or the horse she didn't know. Kate found herself falling and saw the raised hooves of the horse close to her eyes. Her hands began to slip from the bridle and then she felt an agonising blow on her wrist which made her give a cry of pain and let go completely. She felt the ground under her knees and tried to roll clear, but then came another blow on the side of her head which made everything blur and then go black as she dropped into unconsciousness.

Kate came round slowly to feel a foul, insistent throbbing in her head. She gave a little moan, but her throat felt dry, parched, and when she tried to lift her hand to her head it felt like lead. Somebody spoke to her soothingly, reassuringly, but she couldn't understand what they said. Fear came then, the cold prickling fear when you know you're having a nightmare and can't wake up. Desperately she struggled to open her eyes, but when she did everything was blurred and out of focus and great stabs of pain shot through her head, making her give up the struggle and shut them again quickly. But not before she'd realised that a man was bending over her, a man with a lean, bronzed face and very dark hair and eyes. For a terrifying moment she thought that it was part of the dream and the devil had caught her. She gave a little choking whimper of fear and sank thankfully back into oblivion.

When she came round again everything was very different; she was lying on a bed in a cool, white-painted room with the blinds closed to keep out the sun and an air-conditioning plant humming softly in the corner.

From the smell of the place, she knew immediately that she was in a hospital. Tentatively she raised her hand to her head and found a thick dressing on her forehead. Her left arm felt peculiar and when she lifted it she saw that it, too, had been bandaged. Then remembrance came flooding back, all too clearly, and her immediate worry was whether she had managed to save the girl. Fretfully she turned her head on the pillows. Why didn't someone come? She *had* to know what had happened. Her eyes were caught by something dangling from the bed-head and she realised that it was a bell-pull. Quickly she tugged it and waited impatiently for someone to come.

Presently there were the flip-flop sounds of footsteps outside the door and a nurse came bustling in. She spoke slowly, carefully, in English. 'You are awake? Good. You like drink?' Without waiting for an answer she lifted Kate's head and held a glass of liquid to her lips. It was fresh orange juice, bitter, but wonderful to her parched throat.

'Please, where am I?' Kate felt a fool asking such a ham question, but wanted so much to know.

'You in hospital in Palma.' The nurse laid her down again and took her pulse.

'And the girl? The girl on the horse?' Kate asked anxiously. 'Is she all right?'

The nurse looked puzzled for a moment, then her brow cleared. 'Ah, *si*. Is okay.' Then she stuck a thermometer in Kate's mouth so that she had no chance to ask anything more.

When the nurse had gone she closed her eyes again; the pain in her head was just a dull ache now and she guessed that she had been given something to kill the pain. Vaguely she wondered how long she would have to stay here, and remembered with growing unease that you had to pay for medical attention in Spain. There was a soft rap on the door and then she heard it open. As she opened her eyes they grew wide in alarm; the man in the dream was there, the man she had thought to be the devil.

'Please don't be alarmed, *señorita*.' He came nearer and she saw that he was quite young, about twenty-six, and dressed in immaculate riding gear. With a rush of relief she realised who he was. 'How are you feeling now?' he asked with genuine concern.

'A bit woolly,' Kate admitted. 'The girl you were with—is she all right?'

'Perfectly all right, thanks entirely to you, Señorita Selby. I hope you did not mind, I looked in your bag to find your name. In case it was necessary to inform anyone, you understand?'

Kate looked up at him in some puzzlement. His hair was very black and he had the dark, bronzed skin of a Spaniard, but he was much taller than the average male and he spoke English fluently. '*Are* you Spanish?' she asked.

He smiled, revealing even white teeth. 'Yes, but I studied in England for two years.' He gave a graceful little bow. 'I am Carlos de Halmera and the girl you saved is my sister Elena. What you did, *señorita*, was extremely courageous, and I need hardly say that I and my family are forever in your debt and completely at your service.'

Kate flushed. 'It was all I could think of to stop her. I expect it was a silly thing to do really.'

'But very brave.' He picked up her right hand and

carried it to his lips. 'Is there anything at all I can do for you, *señorita*? I was unable to find the address of your hotel, but I expect there will be friends and relations who will be anxious about you.'

Kate turned her head away. 'No, there's no one. I'm here alone, and I'm staying at a private villa, not a hotel.'

'You are alone at the villa?' He sounded incredulous.

She nodded. 'Do you know how long I'll have to stay here?'

'Only until tomorrow. Your wrist is not broken, only sprained, and the doctor here says that you will have a sore head for a while but he will give you some pills to take for it.'

Relieved Kate said, 'Oh, good. I was afraid I wouldn't have enough money to cover. . . .' She broke off as she saw the frown that had come to the Spaniard's face.

'But naturally I will take care of all your expenses, *señorita*. It will be my pleasure and privilege to do so. Do you really think I would allow you to pay yourself when you have saved my sister's life? And I insist that when you leave here tomorrow you accept the hospitality of my house. *Mi casa, su casa.* My house is your house.'

'Oh, but I. . . .'

'Please, *señorita*, don't you see that I cannot allow you to be by yourself when you are still incapacitated?' He indicated her bandaged arm. 'Until you are able to use your hand again you must let me have the honour of taking care of you.'

Kate realised that she had come up against his idea of what was right and proper. He seemed to have be-

come very Spanish, pulling himself stiffly upright, his
head held proudly, and hell-bent on doing his duty by
her whether she liked it or not. And she found that she
did like it, surprisingly. It had been a mistake to shut
herself away completely alone when she was so unhappy and so unsure of herself, and it would be a welcome change to be with other people, especially people
who knew nothing of her reasons for being here.

She gave him a wan smile. 'Okay, Señor de Halmera,
you win. I'll be pleased to stay with you for a few days.
But I'll have to collect my things from the villa—and
I'm expecting a letter too,' she added hurriedly.

'All that will be taken care of,' he told her soothingly.
'If you will give me the address I will send someone to
collect your belongings for you. And I promise that I
will have any letters collected. But now you must rest.
I've kept you too long. *Adiós, señorita.* Until tomorrow.'

And then he was gone, leaving Kate feeling a whole
lot easier in her mind. It would be nice to give herself
over to Carlos de Halmera and his family for a few
days, to be cosseted and have company. It might even
take her mind off Hugo for a while. Hugo. Hugo. Her
heart suddenly cried out to him. How she longed for
him now, to have him by her side, comforting her, instead of Carlos. For him to be as he was before the
wedding, or how she thought he had been, she realised
with bitter irony. Oh, God, would she never stop loving
him, yearning for him? Angrily she turned her face
into the pillows, willing herself not to cry.

Carlos' house was situated in the older part of Palma,
near the ancient cathedral and the Moorish Almudaina

Palace, where the kings of Majorca once lived. He came to collect her in the morning and drove past the magnificent harbour and up a boulevard lined with plane trees before turning off into a narrow side street and halting before high and very heavy iron gates. After he had sounded the horn the gates were opened from within and he drove through a high arched tunnel and into a large courtyard surrounded by windowed walls with the usual little ornate balconies.

Carlos came round to help her solicitously and Kate looked at him in some bewilderment. 'But I thought you must live out in the country,' she remarked. 'Somewhere near where I was staying. Surely you didn't ride all the way out there?'

'No, we have a small hacienda in that area where we go to relax and get away from the town, but our main home is here, as you see.'

He took her elbow and led her up the wide stone steps of a grand outdoor staircase and then through an old wooden door into what Kate could only describe as a reception chamber. It was huge and magnificent, hung with ornate mirrors and chandeliers, and with some beautifully carved chests and other pieces of furniture against the walls. It was also wonderfully cool after the heat of the car.

A door to the right opened and a well-groomed, middle-aged woman came in followed by a young girl who Kate recognised as Elena, and who looked remarkably like her mother. They both hurried forward to greet Kate, hands outstretched and smiles on their faces.

'Señorita Selby, welcome to our house.' They shook her hand and led her into another room where they made her sit down and accept a drink. Talking all the time, thanking her over and over for what she had done, apologising for the injuries she had received, asking how she was, until Kate laughingly insisted they stop.

'Please, it was nothing, and my name is Katherine, but I'm usually called Kate.'

'Katherine is good, *muy bueno*, but Kate I do not like, so we shall call you Katerina,' Señora de Halmera declared comfortably.

They chattered on in their excellent English which made Kate quite ashamed of her meagre Spanish, and she gathered that the head of the family, Señor Alfonso, was away on the mainland on a business trip. It seemed that the family had taken full advantage of the tourist boom to build a great many hotels, not only in Majorca and the other Balearic islands, but on the mainland coasts as well; Señor Alfonso always going to Spain for several weeks at a time in the summer to oversee the running of these while Carlos stayed to take care of those on the islands.

After a light lunch, they made her rest for the whole of the afternoon and she was shown into a large room overlooking an inner courtyard where a fountain spouted from a cornucopia held by a fat bronze cherub, and where flowers of every colour and scent ran riot in window boxes, hanging baskets and huge ornamental terracotta tubs. She found that her things had been brought from the villa as promised, and had already been neatly unpacked for her. The family, she realised, must be loaded, but there was no pretentiousness about them, probably because the money had always been there. They were kind and friendly and overwhelmingly grateful to her for Elena's escape.

During the next couple of days she had several sharp, stabbing headaches, but the pills she had been given proved effective and she only had to rest in a darkened room for a half hour or so and they went away. On her second day Señora de Halmera took her back to the hospital where they removed the dressings, leaving her with just an elastic bandage on her wrist and a plaster over the cut on her forehead, which was so high up that she was able to hide it altogether by combing her hair over it.

On the third day of her stay with the Majorcan family, Señora de Halmera had to go out and Elena was at school, so Carlos came home from his office early especially to drive her to see their hacienda and for Kate to make sure that the villa was all right; she was rather worried about all those electrical gadgets being left on with no one there. Carlos had an Italian sports car, a convertible, and Kate thoroughly enjoyed the drive. She felt completely at ease with Carlos now, he was only four years older than her, and since he had lived in England, they were pretty much on the same wavelength. He wasn't beyond eyeing her appreciatively, but otherwise treated her with the exemplary manners that a well-bred Spaniard always shows a guest.

Before going to his hacienda he took her for a drive up into the mountains, up the serpentine road with its thirty-eight hairpins to stop at one or two *miradors*, viewpoints where they stood and gazed at the unforgettable panoramas of the cliffs tumbling sheer into the deep, clear blue of the Mediterranean. He took her off the tourist track to out-of-the-way villages and showed her ancient sanctuaries and calvaries, and once a still-used and very busy monastery high on a hill, a white building with green shutters and a huge, ornate crown on the roof. They passed fields where straw-hatted peasants of both sexes had stretched nets or sheets out on the ground under the trees and were beating the branches vigorously with long sticks. When Kate exclaimed in astonishment, Carlos laughed and told her that they were knocking the ripe almonds from the trees and catching them in the nets, ready to be picked up by a lorry. He told her that often the fields were some way from the farms, but now the peasants were well enough off to drive there in their cars or on noisy mopeds—Med-peds, Carlos called them.

The hacienda, too, was a surprise. She had expected quite a small place from Carlos' description, but he drove through high pillars set in a sandstone wall and hung with heavy wrought-iron gates. Rows of tall, closely-packed cypresses formed an inner wall round the boundary of the property, and set in the centre was a long, low, white-painted house which had a Moorish look to it with its arched doors and windows and tiled floors.

'Why, Carlos, this is perfect!' she exclaimed in delight. 'I feel as if I ought to be in Africa instead of Spain.'

'Yes, we owe much of our architecture to the Moors who ruled here for many years, and it is ideally suited to a hot climate.'

He showed her round the stables and pointed out the terraces of orange and lemon groves owned by his family, and which seemed to stretch almost as far as they could see. Later they rested in the cool of the house and sat sipping frosted drinks in long glasses and listening to records, mostly American and English, but also some Spanish guitar music which Kate took to at once.

'If you like guitar music then you must go to a bar in Palma that has a very good player. I will take you there, if you would like it.'

'It sounds great. I'd love to go. When?'

'Whenever you wish, but if you don't mind, not tonight.'

'Got a date already?'

He grinned rather wryly. 'Yes, with Consuelo Muchia, a neighbour of ours.' Suddenly he turned to her and said in a rush, 'But she's like you—very independent—and she wishes to take up a career, to be liberated.' His lip definitely curled for a moment. 'Whenever I try to pin her down she refuses to give me a straight answer,' he added angrily.

'Maybe that's the trouble,' Kate said quietly. 'There are some girls who don't like to be trapped and pinned down like a butterfly in a glass case. They want to be free to go where they please.'

'To go from man to man as a butterfly goes from flower to flower, I suppose,' Carlos replied sardonically.

'Not necessarily. Just because a girl doesn't want to get married, it doesn't follow that she's promiscuous,' Kate returned tartly, a definite edge to her voice.

Carlos immediately looked contrite. 'I beg your pardon, Katerina. Please don't think that I meant to imply.... It is different for English girls, I know. They have already learnt how to cope with emancipation. But as for Consuelo....' He shrugged exasperatedly. 'She thinks she needs to be free, but she wouldn't know what to do with herself if she was.' He stared brood-

ingly at his drink while Kate sat silently watching
him. Then he became aware of her regard and immediately apologised. 'It was wrong of me to inflict my
troubles on you. And we had better leave now if you
want to check on the villa before we go back to Palma.'

But apart from having to throw out some food that
had become stale, the villa was perfectly all right. Kate
remembered to look in the green-painted letterbox
fixed to the gatepost at the end of the driveway, but it
was still empty.

As they drove back towards Palma, she wondered if
this was because of the slowness of the Spanish postal
system or whether Simon and Margie just didn't have
any news for her. Worriedly she tried to work out what
Hugo's reaction would be; whether he would still want
his revenge—make her pay, as he called it—or whether,
after thinking it over, he would just simply want to be
free of her, wash his hands of the whole episode.

They were driving now through the busy main street
of the small town where she had gone to do her shopping soon after she had arrived at the villa, and it
could only have been because she had been thinking of
Hugo that suddenly a man walking along the crowded
pavement looked exactly like him! He was walking
briskly along, threading his way through the crowds
who partly hid him from her view, but she saw that
he appeared to be searching for someone, his head turning all the time to look around him. Kate's heart gave a
great, breath-stopping lurch and she closed her eyes
tight for a moment before opening them again to take
another look.

For a second the man seemed to be staring right at
her, the sunlight reflected on the lenses of his sun-

glasses, then a party of tourists stepped in front of him, obscuring him. Kate craned her neck to look back as Carlos drove past, then gave a heartfelt sigh of relief. It wasn't Hugo; the man had joined the group of tourists and was talking with them, his back towards her. Kate settled back in her seat, her heart still pounding, her hands shaking, and took herself severely to task. She'd end up as a nervous wreck if she kept seeing Hugo's double in every tall, dark man that happened to walk by. Especially in a country full of dark-haired men!

CHAPTER FOUR

ALTHOUGH Kate was loath to admit it, the outing that afternoon had tired her and she was glad enough to go to bed early, but towards midnight she awoke feeling hot and sticky. Crossing to the window, she leaned out over the little balcony and listened to the distant sound of the sea breaking gently against the harbour walls, no great booming ocean roar this, but the tideless lapping of an almost landlocked sea. There was another sound of water too, the musical tinkling of the fountain that played in the inner patio below her window, suggesting a coolness which drew her irresistibly to push her feet into lacy mules, to slip a negligee over her nightdress, and to make her way through the darkened house into the comparative freshness of the courtyard.

A canopied garden seat stood in one corner near a great spray of purple bougainvillaea, its scent heavy and cloying on the night air, and here Kate sat, her feet tucked under her, too restless to sleep yet too tired to read. The chance glimpse of the man who resembled Hugo had unnerved her more than she cared to admit; being among people who knew nothing about him had begun to help a little and the hurt of his betrayal hadn't been quite such a raw and open wound over the last two days—not that it had started to heal, but she hadn't been constantly aware of it at every moment of the day. But just seeing that man——!

Kate gripped the arm of the chair tightly. It was no

good; she had followed the first instinct of any wounded thing, to get as far away as possible from the source of hurt, but she had been in Majorca for a week now and it hadn't helped. Miserably she wondered if it would have been better to have stayed in London and faced up to things. But the very thought of facing Hugo when he was so blazingly angry, so vindictive, made her cringe. No, that first instinct at least had been right. It had been one of pure self-preservation, because he'd looked as if he could cheerfully have strangled her. But surely by now he would have had time to cool down, to look at the whole episode more objectively, see that it would be better to wipe the slate clean and go their separate ways, each of them disillusioned in the other.

She was just on the point of going back to bed having made up her mind to telephone Simon at his office the following morning to find out if anything had developed, when she heard a door banging and then the light snapped on in the room opening on to the patio. Through the opened doors she saw Carlos pouring himself a stiff drink before he walked moodily into the patio, his shoulders hunched morosely.

'Hi.' He jumped when she let him know that she was there and came over to her corner. 'Had a good time?' she ventured.

Carlos bent to switch on a lamp and joined her on the seat, his legs stretched out and looking very moody and handsome in his black evening suit as he glowered into his drink.

'No, I didn't,' he said shortly. 'Consuelo wanted to go home early because she has to prepare for a lecture she's attending tomorrow.'

'Midnight is hardly early,' Kate put in mildly.

'It is in Spain; we keep late hours here. But anyway, she wanted to go home even before this, but I managed to persuade her to stay on for a while longer.'

He swallowed his drink and then got up to stride up and down the courtyard in frustration. 'Tonight I asked her again to name a date for our wedding, but she always refuses to give me a definite answer. It's always, "There's plenty of time", or "Perhaps next year". And every time my father comes home he wants to know why the marriage is not yet settled, tells me I should be more firm with her. But I'm not like him, Katerina. I've tried to be patient with Consuelo, given her time to make up her mind.' He came closer again and said passionately, 'I'm not an old-fashioned Spanish martinet. If Consuelo really wanted a career more than anything else, if I thought she didn't really love me, then believe me, I wouldn't try to stand in her way. But I honestly don't think that's the case. She just doesn't seem to know her own mind. She's read books and talked to some of her friends, and now she thinks that she too. . . .' He broke off abruptly and ran a hand through his hair. 'I'm sorry, I must be boring you with my problems.'

Kate said slowly, 'Sometimes, for some people, it helps to talk things out. How long have you known Consuelo?'

He shrugged eloquently. 'All our lives. Our families have been connected by marriage and by common business interests for the last hundred years.'

'Perhaps that's half the trouble,' she said gently, realising just how much this meant to him. 'You've always been around and she takes it for granted that you always will be. She knows you love her, so she can come back to you if the career idea falls through.'

Throwing himself moodily into a chair, Carlos said bitterly, 'So I'm to be second best, a last resort?'

'Well, there's one sure way to make her come to a decision, one way or the other.'

Carlos looked at her quickly. 'There is?'

Kate smiled a little. 'Of course. Make her jealous. If she loves you she'll realise what she's losing and name the day at once. If she doesn't—well, that's a chance you have to take.'

'And one I'm willing to take. But it wouldn't work, Katerina, because we live in a small community here and it wouldn't be fair of me to pay attention to another girl when I have no intention of marrying her. It would be quite unthinkable and could even lead to a rift between families.'

'Well, isn't there anyone else? Someone who's family doesn't live here? There must be lots of girls who work in your hotels.'

'Yes, there are, but I doubt if Consuelo would be taken in by one of them, she wouldn't believe that I was serious.'

'Then I'm afraid that I can't help you. You'll just have to exert all your masculine charms and persuade her that marriage to you will be more exciting than doing her own thing,' Kate said rather tiredly. 'If you'll excuse me I think I'll go back to bed, I think I could sleep again now.' She moved to walk back into the house, her figure silhouetted in the light of the lamp, her long red-gold hair tousled round her face.

'Katerina!' The sudden urgency in Carlos' voice made her stop and look back.

'Yes, what is it?'

'I think that perhaps there is one way you can help me. One that would add exceedingly to the already great debt my family owe you.'

There was an excited glint in his expressive eyes and in a moment of intuition she guessed what he wanted of her. 'Oh, no!'

'But, yes, Katerina. Can you not see?' he asked eagerly. 'It would be perfect. You are not a Spanish girl so you have no family who would be offended, you are a guest in my home so Consuelo would know that I see you often, and you have no feelings for me so would not be hurt by pretending to like me. And most of all,' he paused, 'most of all, you are so very lovely that no man could help but fall for you.'

'Oh, no,' Kate said again. 'Look, Carlos, I don't want to get involved with any arguments with your girl-friend. Just forget the whole thing, will you? It was a crazy idea and I'm sorry I suggested it. And it wouldn't have worked anyway; as you said, she would see through it in a minute.'

'But it *will* work, Katerina. With your help. You're so beautiful that the moment she sees you she'll just have to believe it.'

He went on trying to persuade her and Kate realised unhappily just what she'd let herself in for. She held up her hands to silence him. 'Okay, okay. Just be quiet for a moment and let me think. Look, I'll tell you what I'll do,' she said after a few minutes while Carlos stood obediently silent beside her. 'I'll agree to help you only so long as you agree to set Consuelo free to follow a career if it doesn't work.'

He nodded at once. 'I've already said that I won't force her to marry me; I meant it, Katerina.'

She looked at him searchingly, then nodded, satisfied. 'All right. Then I think it would be best if you set a few rumours going round about us first. That will make her uncertain and she may try to meet me, but it will be best if she sees us together. Can you arrange that?'

'Easily. A neighbour of ours has taken over a local nightclub to give an engagement party for his daughter in a few days' time. Consuelo will of course be going, and I will escort you there.'

'That sounds all right, but you mustn't overdo it, Carlos, or she'll see through it.'

He grinned devilishly. 'Don't worry, I think I know just how to handle it.'

'Well, I hope so, because you'll only get the one chance. I—I may have to go back to England pretty soon.'

'But your arm is not yet completely healed. And you have seen little of our island as yet,' he protested.

Kate merely shook her head, too tired suddenly to want to argue. 'We'll talk about it some other time. Goodnight, Carlos—and don't blame me if Consuelo thinks you're fickle and refuses to have anything more to do with you ever again.'

He laughed. 'Goodnight, Katerina, and thank you.' He took her hand and gave her a slight bow, but when she went to draw it away he wouldn't let go. She looked at him and found him watching her quizzically. 'Katerina, don't you think it would be a good idea if we practised a little before we—er—flirted with each other in public? Just so that we get it right, you understand?'

Kate had to laugh. 'No, I don't. Carlos, you're incorrigible!' She freed her hand and turned back into the house leaving him alone on the patio.

During the next few days Señora de Halmera took it on herself to show Kate the island, taking her not only to the more popular tourist areas but also to the age-old heart of Majorca to see the secluded villages and villas set in terraced orange and olive groves beneath the pine trees that nestled in the foothills of the spectacular range of mountains. During the weekend Carlos and Elena accompanied them and then they explored sleepy fishing villages bordering the bay of Alcudia on the northern side of the island, and picnicked aboard a hired rowing boat among the fascinating marshes of Albufera, a lonely haunt unknown to tourists, where hundreds of wildfowl nested and where they saw egrets, exotic flamingoes and the glossy ibis.

Carlos took her aside on Sunday evening and told her that their plan was well in hand; he had sounded her praises in a few receptive ears and was sure that they'd got to Consuelo because she had phoned him on some pretext and said that she'd heard they had an English girl staying with them.

'I was very discreet,' he told Kate exultantly. 'I pretended I didn't want to talk about you, which made her more curious than ever. Katerina, I'm sure it's going to work!'

'Well, let's hope so. But don't build your hopes up too high,' she warned.

But Kate, too, was feeling a little easier in her mind. She had managed to get through to Simon and he'd told her that he'd received an answer from Hugo's solicitors that very morning. But it merely said that Hugo was still considering what course of action to take and would let them know in due course. So that was that. She was still in the same position, but somehow the urgency seemed to have been taken from the situation by his matter-of-fact reply, and she was able to relax a little and enjoy her outings with the Halmeras.

On the day of the engagement party she was to attend with Carlos, Kate went shopping with Señora de Halmera. They went to the usual places: the bank, a couple of dress shops, a hairdressing salon, and ended up in a restaurant where Señora de Halmera, who was already very comfortably rounded, tucked into several cream cakes. Kate watched her enviously and sipped lemon tea. They had the table by the window and the older woman was kept busy waving to acquaintances who passed by. But suddenly she broke off some story she was relating to say angrily, 'There he is again! Really, it is too much the way he follows and stares at us!'

Kate looked at her in some bewilderment. 'Who? Who's staring?'

'That man over there. You see—the one with the grey suit and a camera round his neck.'

She pointed across the busy road to a palm-treed square where a man leant against a lamp-post, his hands in his pockets, gazing across at them. Kate recognised him at once. It was the man who had taken her photograph when she'd been shopping near the villa.

'You say he's been following us, *señora*?'

'Yes, I've noticed him twice before: once when we were having lunch at Valledemosa up in the mountains, and again when we were with Elena and Carlos at the weekend.' She frowned in annoyance. 'I shall tell Carlos to inform the police. It is too much!'

'I'm afraid it may be my fault,' Kate told her unhappily. 'He took my photograph when I first came here and he may have got a crush on me—you know, like watching me. It's happened to me once or twice before, and to several of my friends. Someone sees your photograph in a magazine or on a poster and finds out who you are. Then they follow you and just—just look at you. Play out some fantasy or other in their minds, I suppose. Usually they're quite harmless, and you can only hope that eventually they'll fall for someone else and leave you alone.'

Señora de Halmera looked shocked. 'And you have to put up with this?'

Kate shrugged. 'What else can you do? They're not breaking any laws if they don't try to molest you. It may not be pleasant, but you just have to look on it as an occupational hazard, I'm afraid.'

Sure enough, much to the Señora's irritation, when they left the restaurant the man followed them at a distance, keeping them in sight but making no attempt to approach them.

And he was there again when she drove out to go to the party that evening with Carlos, which didn't help her nerves any. She wasn't looking forward to the party, feeling that there was something underhand in the trick they were going to play on the unknown Consuelo. Still, she supposed it would be justified if it led to the girl's eventual happiness. She had dressed very carefully for the part she was to play, wearing one of the new creations she had bought for her trousseau. It was a clinging black sheath with a wide, slit neckline, and with long tight sleeves that covered the crêpe bandage on her wrist, and which made her look very feminine but hid none of her curves. Her hair she wore smoothed close to her head on the crown, then fluffed out into loose curls all round her head.

Carlos looked very debonair in his dinner suit, the whiteness of his dress shirt heightening his tanned skin. As he remarked, they made a striking couple, one to whom all eyes would inevitably be drawn. And they were, in fact, an immediate focus of attention. Only one bar of the night-club was open to the public that evening, the rest had been taken over by the parents of the engaged couple, and Kate was one of the few foreigners there. Her fair skin and hair alone made her stand out from the other women and she was soon surrounded by a crowd of Carlos' friends who demanded to be introduced to her. This he did, but taking care to keep a proprietorial arm round her waist and taking her off to dance before anyone else had the chance to ask her.

'Which is Consuelo?' Kate hissed at him as they danced round.

He pulled her a little nearer to him and whispered in her ear, 'She's sitting at the table over by the door. Wearing a blue dress.'

Kate peeped over his shoulder and found the one he meant; a dark-haired girl with large, long-lashed eyes and full red lips, her head set proudly on her shapely figure. And at the moment her eyes were watching them intently as Carlos continued to hold Kate close.

'But, Carlos, she's beautiful!'

'Do you think I don't know that? Now you see why she wouldn't have believed it if I'd pretended to fall for someone else,' he hissed back at her, his mouth close to her ear.

Suddenly Kate began to giggle. 'She looks as if she'd

like to murder us. If she only knew what we were say-ing! All this just for her benefit.'

Carlos too began to laugh and they were still chuck-ling with amusement when they came off the floor. He brought her a drink and danced two more dances with her before he reluctantly relinquished her to one of his friends. Only then did he go over to Consuelo and ask her to dance. Kate tried to watch them over her partner's shoulder, but kept getting her view blocked by other couples. When she did get near enough to observe them she almost laughed aloud, for Carlos, al-though bending his head to listen politely to Consuelo, was making it perfectly obvious that his attention wasn't on her, his eyes going constantly round the room to find Kate. And when he did find her he gave her a long, lingering look of admiration. His partner went on talking, but the smile on her face had become some-what fixed and she shot a rather venomous look across the room at Kate. At the end of the dance Carlos made it appear as if he could hardly wait to get back to her, hurrying across the room to claim her from her partner and find a table for them in a quiet corner, but one that was also positioned where Consuelo could see them quite clearly, even though she was pretending not to.

There was a cabaret then, during which Carlos sat close to her, his arm negligently across the back of her chair, his fingers idly toying with her hair.

Kate turned to him with a dazzling smile. 'Do you think it's working?'

'Yes, I'm sure of it. She asked me if I'd take her sailing soon, but I made an excuse and said I was busy.' He brushed her cheek with his lips. 'But I don't think it would do any harm if we made it a little bit more obvious.'

Raising an eyebrow, Kate whispered, 'How obvious can you get?'

He grinned. 'You'll see!'

After the cabaret everyone drank a toast to the engaged couple and there were a few speeches before they could get back to the serious business of the evening. The beat became more sensuous as the lights dimmed and Carlos led her on to the floor again. He drew her into his arms and held her closely but gently, as if he was afraid she might break if he held her too tightly. They danced slowly round the room, his lips brushing her hair, seemingly oblivious of everyone else in the place. Kate tried to look for Consuelo but could see little in the darkened room with Carlos' broad shoulders in the way, but then she saw Consuelo being led on to the floor by a young Spaniard.

'She's dancing,' she whispered to Carlos.

'*Bueno.*'

Steering her to where French doors stood open to a terrace hung with trailing plants and large potted shrubs, he led her out there and they stood close together in the moonlight, framed by the doorway.

'Can you see them?' Kate asked him.

'No, not yet.' Carlos craned his neck to see. 'They're just coming in sight. Now!' He bent his head and drew her to him, his shoulders hunched in a passionate embrace as he pretended to kiss her.

Kate hoped it looked good for Carlos' sake, but the whole situation was so ridiculous that she began to giggle again.

'Stop it,' Carlos mumbled at her, his lips close to hers.

'Can't help it,' she mumbled back between her teeth.

But then he made her stop because he kissed her properly, taking her by surprise so that she was unable to resist and break free from him for several minutes.

'Hey, that wasn't part of the bargain,' she reproved him.

He grinned, his teeth gleaming white in the semi-darkness. 'I had to make it look good. Consuelo knows I can do better than that.'

'Does she indeed? And I thought all Spanish girls were supposed to be prim and proper. Can we go back in now?'

'It would be better if we stayed out here a little longer, but we can move out of the doorway now, she's gone by.' He led her to the edge of the terrace and they stood leaning against the parapet gazing out at the sea just a few hundred yards away. 'Would you like a drink?'

'Mm, please. But you'll give the game away if you go back in, won't you?'

'No, I can go into the other bar.'

He went away and Kate turned back to look out at the waves lapping gently on the shore, their white crests turned to a phosphorescent silver in the moonlight. In the nightclub the band swept into the fast, rather noisy rhythm of a pop number, the vocalist belting it out for all she was worth.

Kate heard a footstep behind her and half turned. 'Carlos?'

The voice that answered her was very familiar—but not the one she expected. 'Who's Carlos? Another one of your lovers?'

For a moment Kate stood as though turned to stone, unable to believe her own ears, every emotion, every sense suspended, feeling nothing but the beating of her own heart that seemed to have swelled until it threatened to burst through her chest. It couldn't be! It couldn't! But even as she turned slowly, oh, so slowly, to face him, she knew that it was true. Hugo stood just a few feet away from her, his face partly in shadow, only his eyes, lightened by some cruel trick of the moon, betrayed his malicious triumph. He seemed to have sprung out of the night, to be a creature of it in his black evening suit and with his dark hair and grey eyes. Kate felt her legs begin to give way and she stepped hastily back to lean against the wall, her nails desperately digging into the soft brickwork.

'Who's Carlos?' he said again, his voice harsh and relentless. 'Some other poor devil you've hooked on your line?'

From somewhere Kate found the strength to speak. 'H-how did you find me?' she managed, her voice tight and unnatural.

'That we can talk about later,' he answered unpleasantly. 'Right now there are one or two other things I want to discuss with you. But not here. I'm taking you to a place where you and I can be quite alone. After all, that's what all newlyweds want, isn't it, to be alone together?' His voice was hard and threatening behind the edge of mockery.

'No!' Kate was panicked into movement. 'I'm not going anywhere with you!' She tried to hurry past him towards the light and noise coming from the nightclub. 'You have no right to....'

'No right!' His coldness was suddenly gone. His eyes

blazed at her savagely and he moved to corner her against the wall, looming over her like a lean and powerful animal. 'You *dare* to say I have no right. You little bitch! I have every right to do what I damn well want to you.' His hand came out to grip her throat, his fingers biting into her flesh.

Kate screamed. Just once. Because then his hand had covered her mouth and he was pulling her towards some steps that led down to the back of the building. Desperately she tried to break free, tearing at his hand with her nails. Hugo swore at her and tightened his grip on her arm. But then she heard a shout behind her and suddenly she was set free as Carlos came running up.

'Katerina, what is it? Was this man hurting you?'

She tried to gather her scattered wits, but before she could answer, Hugo said smoothly, 'Certainly not. Katherine and I were just going out for a stroll along the beach, that's all. Come along.' He reached out to take her arm again, but Kate shrank back.

'That isn't true! He was forcing me to go.'

Two of Carlos' friends had come out now and they came to join in the group, giving her an increased sense of safety.

'Don't be silly, Kate. You know we have to have that little talk,' Hugo said imperatively.

Puzzled, Carlos asked, 'Do you know this man, Katerina?'

Slowly Kate turned to look at Hugo as he gazed back at her sardonically. She said clearly, 'I never saw him before in my life.'

'Why, you lying little....' He lunged forward and caught her by her left wrist, dragging her towards the steps. His fingers dug in cruelly, biting into the already bruised flesh beneath the crêpe bandage, and Kate gave a cry of agony, waves of nausea sweeping over her as the pain deepened.

There was a confusion of noise and movement around her and then she found herself sitting in a chair with Carlos leaning over her anxiously, his hair and clothes dishevelled.

'That man? Has he gone?' It was her only coherent thought.

'*Sí.* Don't worry. He was a gatecrasher, we threw him out.' He held a drink out to her and she swallowed it down, her hand shaking so much that she spilled some on her dress. Other people had gathered round her and she said urgently, 'Carlos, I'm sorry if it upsets your plans, but please, I've got to go home.'

'*Desde luego.* But of course.' Solicitously he collected her bag for her and helped her along. Everyone was very kind, very upset that such a thing should have happened at a private party. They would have asked her questions, commiserated with her, but Kate just wanted to get away and looked beseechingly at Carlos. He came to her rescue at once and took her out to his car, two other young men coming with them in case the 'gatecrasher' was still hanging round, but there was no sign of Hugo as they drove away.

Kate kept glancing behind them, wondering anxiously if they were being followed, but there was so much traffic about she couldn't be sure one way or the other, and she couldn't be easy until the heavy iron doors of the Halmera house had clanged shut behind them.

'Katerina, you look so pale. Did that man frighten you very much?'

'No, it wasn't that. He pulled my bad wrist.' No need to tell him that Hugo's very presence had frightened her to death.

Carlos gave an angry exclamation. 'If I had known that we would have made sure he regretted it before we threw him out. I'll get some water so that you can soak your wrist.'

'It's all right, I'll do it when I go up to my room. But I would like another drink, please, I still feel a bit shaky.'

'Of course.' He poured her out a large brandy in a delicate balloon and gave it to her. 'Katerina, you said you didn't know that man, and yet he called you by your name?' he said with a frown between his brows.

'Yes, but not until you'd already used it,' Kate replied steadily.

The frown cleared. 'That's true. But he knew you were English?'

'Perhaps he heard us talking together,' Kate answered rather impatiently. 'Does it matter?'

'No, of course not,' Carlos said quickly when he saw she was upset. 'He must have come out from the other bar when he saw that I'd left you alone.'

'Did you—did you hurt him very much?' she asked with difficulty.

Carlos shrugged expressively. 'It was necessary to use some force to get rid of him, yes. He put up quite a fight and it took several of us to finally overpower him. But I think he'll have quite a few bruises too tomorrow,' he added with some satisfaction as he looked at his scraped knuckles.

'Oh.' Kate received this news with mixed feelings, but part of her was definitely pleased, because she'd have liked nothing better than to sock Hugo in the eye too. She finished her drink and rose to her feet. 'If you don't mind I think I'll go up to my room now. It's still early yet, why don't you go back to the party?'

'And ruin our plan? Consuelo wouldn't think me very enamoured of you if I left you alone after this, would she?'

'Good heavens, I'd forgotten all about that. Did it work, do you think?'

'I'm almost certain of it. But we won't know for sure until she tries to get in touch with me.'

'And when she does?'

He made a little moue with his lips. 'Well, perhaps I might punish her a little more. After all, she's kept me waiting for quite long enough.'

'Well, don't play too hard to get or she may go to someone else on the rebound,' Kate said drily.

'Oh, I shan't do that. Consuelo's mine and no one else shall have her if I can prevent it.'

Kate looked at him for a moment and then turned tiredly to go to her bedroom. For all his claims to being emancipated, Carlos was still the dictatorial male his ancestors were at heart. Which was probably why she had quelled her first instinct to confide in him, to tell him who Hugo really was. If he had known that he might not have been so willing to get Hugo away from her. She took off the crêpe bandage and soaked her wrist in a basin of cold water, the flesh red and angry where Hugo's fingers had dug into her. Looking at it, she realised that she would carry the marks of his anger for some time to come.

Wearily she wondered what on earth she was going to do. She was sure that now Hugo had found her he wouldn't let her go again. He wouldn't rest until he'd got her in his power to exact the revenge he had so violently sworn to take. Kate shivered in genuine fear. Suppose he came to the house and told them that she was his wife, demanded to have her returned to him? Would Carlos let him take her? She wasn't sure, didn't know how far she could trust him in the circumstances. Perhaps she ought to leave here now; go to the airport, get a plane to England, anywhere! But then the moment of blind panic passed and she gave herself a mental shake. Of course she could trust Carlos. She'd saved Elena from a nasty accident, hadn't she? He owed her his protection for that reason, if nothing else. And she wouldn't hesitate to use it if Hugo tried to come after her. No, she was safer here. Safe so long as she stayed inside the high walls of the old house, or kept with the others when they went out. Hugo couldn't very well try to kidnap her in broad daylight, although he'd tried to do near enough that tonight. Then a new fear came; she couldn't stay here for ever, she'd have to leave some time.

But this thought was pushed resolutely from her mind. Sufficient unto the day. Miserably she climbed into the high wooden bed, knowing already that it would be impossible to sleep. Hugo had looked so angry, so cruel, his eyes ruthless, his face implacable. And she loved him so much. So much that even the pain in her wrist was an exquisite kind of agony because he had caused it.

Next day the family fussed over her, although Kate could tell that Señora de Halmera wasn't very happy about the incident. To have a man following them and then for Kate to be molested all in the same day was a little too much for her to take with equanimity. So Kate stayed quietly in the house all day and refused another, rather half-hearted, invitation from the Señora to go shopping in Palma again with her. She did, however, ask for permission to use the phone and waited impatiently for the connection to Simon's office. As usual, the lines out of Majorca were all engaged and there was a long delay.

She tried to read an English paperback that Carlos had bought for her, but she couldn't settle to it; she kept remembering the way Hugo had looked at her the previous night. After a while she gave up the attempt and wandered through the beautifully furnished rooms of the house. Idly she went to a window that overlooked the street and leaned out over the balcony. If she craned her head she could just see the harbour where a cruise liner was disgorging boatloads of passengers, all eager to see the sights of the capital. At the bottom of the street a man led along a mule, a straw hat fitted over its ears, and across its back two panniers laden with brightly painted peasant pottery, a lure for the free-spending tourists. A car turned into the street from the main boulevard and stopped a little way further along. A man stepped into the sunlight from the deep shadow of an alleyway almost opposite the house and went over to the car. It was the Spaniard who had been following her. He said something to the driver of the car, gesticulating in the direction of the house as he did so. Somehow it came as no surprise when Hugo got out of the car and stood looking up at her.

Kate just stood there, unable to move, until the telephone ringing behind her made her jump and brought her back to her senses. Quickly she picked up the receiver and with relief heard Simon's voice.

Without preamble she said urgently, 'Simon, he's found me. He's here now. He's outside the house this very minute!' Her voice rose in mounting panic.

'Has he said anything? Told you what he wants to do?'

'Oh, Simon, please try to understand; he's in no mood to talk! All he wants to do is get his own back on me because he thinks I lied to him. And don't advise me to tell him the truth,' she went on before he could answer, 'because he wouldn't listen, and wouldn't believe me anyway.'

'All right, now try to keep calm. Try to look at it sensibly. Are you safe from him at the moment?'

'Yes, I suppose so. But I can't impose on the Halmeras' hospitality for much longer. I've been here a week already.'

'Does he know about the villa, do you think?'

'No, I don't see how he could. But I'd really rather come back to England. Can't you get a court order or something to make him stay away from me?'

'Yes, I could, but it would bring everything out into the open. Look, leave it with me for a while, Kate. I'll get on to his solicitor and threaten him with the court order unless Merrion returns to England and promises to leave you alone. The fear of a scandal might do the trick. I expect they know where to contact him, so I'll insist they tell him today. Give me your number and I'll call you back later tonight.'

'All right, but please hurry, Simon. I can't stand much more of this.'

She gave him the number and rang off. It took her quite a while before she found the courage to go to the window again and look out. Hugo and the car had gone, but the other man was still there in the shadows, watching, like a fox who waits for the rabbit to come out of its hole.

Carlos came home to lunch announcing that he had taken the afternoon off to catch up on some household accounts, but during the afternoon Consuelo was shown into the room where Kate was helping Señora de Halmera to match up some embroidery silks for an altar-cloth she was repairing for the cathedral.

'I hope you are recovering from the attack on you yesterday,' Consuelo said to Kate after they had been formally introduced. 'It was most unfortunate.'

'Thank you, I'm fine now. It was kind of you to ask.'

The Spanish girl turned to talk to Señora de Halmera, but she kept giving little puzzled looks in Kate's direction. Probably wondering if I really am a femme fatale out to steal her boy-friend, Kate thought wryly

Somebody must have tipped Carlos off that Consuelo was here, because he came in soon after she had arrived, greeting her politely but smiling warmly at Kate and coming to sit beside her.

Señora de Halmera couldn't help but notice. She gave them an uneasy glance and said, 'Carlos, Consuelo will be interested to see those paintings that we have had restored and cleaned. Will you show them to her?'

'*Si, madre.*'

He excused himself to Kate and escorted Consuelo out of the room. When they had gone, the Señora said carefully, 'Carlos and Consuelo are very old friends. In fact we hope that they will marry quite soon.'

'Yes, I know. Carlos told me.'

The Señora looked surprised, but after a moment went on slowly, 'Consuelo telephoned me earlier to-day. She was rather worried. She thought that perhaps you and Carlos ... that Carlos was attracted to you.' She bent to pick up a bright red skein of silk. 'I must tell you, *señorita*, that this match has the approval and blessing of both families. We would not want anything to prevent it, you understand?'

'Oh, yes, I understand completely.' So Carlos hadn't told his mother of his plan to make Consuelo jealous. Well, if he hadn't confided in her it was hardly Kate's place to do so. Which left her with only one thing to do. She stood up. 'If you'll excuse me I'll go and pack my things at once. Perhaps you'd be kind enough to let me use the phone to arrange a flight?'

'But of course. I am sorry, Katerina,' Señora de Halmera seemed genuinely upset. 'We owe you so much for saving Elena, but if Carlos....' She broke off, look-ing at Kate unhappily.

'Please don't worry, *señora*. You've been very kind to me, and it's time I was leaving anyhow.'

But when she was left alone and spoke to the airline, Kate was unable to book a seat on a return flight for two days. So now what? She couldn't stay here, that was certain, not after Consuelo had spoken to the Señora. So that left a hotel or the villa. The thought of a hotel, where anyone could walk in or out with im-punity, she hardly considered for more than a minute. She would be much too vulnerable there. But how to get to the villa without being followed?

While she was still pondering the problem Carlos came in, a triumphant glint in his eyes telling her that their ploy had worked even before he opened his mouth.

'September the ninth,' he said exultantly. 'She's set a date at last!'

'Well, bully for you,' she said sardonically.

He looked surprised. 'But, Katerina, are you not glad for me? It is all thanks to you.'

'And thanks to you, your mother's virtually asked me to leave. Why didn't you tell her what we planned to do?'

'But I couldn't. She would have forbidden us to go ahead with it.'

'Well, Consuelo told her what we were up to last night and now I'm persona non grata as far as she's concerned.'

To Carlos' credit he looked genuinely shocked. 'But, Katerina, you must stay as long as you like. I will go to my mother at once and explain. I just hope that she won't feel she has to tell Consuelo the truth.'

He turned to go, but Kate called him back. 'Thanks, Carlos, but it really is time I left here anyway. I can manage quite well with my wrist now. I've booked a flight back to England, but the earliest one I could get isn't for two days.' She held up a hand as he went to speak. 'It's all right, I can go back to the villa until then. But I'm worried about that man who's been following me. I'm afraid he may trail me there. Is there any way we can get rid of him?'

'Of course. Leave him to me.'

Two hours later Carlos was driving her out of Palma,

past the airport and out towards the mountains, and to Kate's relief there was no one following them. He had merely phoned the police and they had taken the man away. It had been that simple.

He was very happy during the drive, telling her how Consuelo had burst into tears and asked him to forgive her, promising to marry him as soon as he liked. Privately Kate thought that the girl must have been on the verge of doing so already if she had been so easily persuaded, but perhaps it had needed that little push to make her know her own mind once and for all.

'I'll come and pick you up and take you to the airport in time for your flight,' Carlos promised. 'You're sure you'll be all right alone at the villa?'

'Yes, fine, thanks. Oh, but I was expecting a phone call from my—from a friend tonight. Will you tell him where I am and ask him to meet me at Gatwick when I land?'

'Of course.' He drove up the quiet track to the villa and took out her cases and a large basket of fruit and groceries that his mother had insisted she take with her. 'You're sure there's nothing else I can do for you?'

'Quite sure. You'd better get back or Consuelo will think I've kidnapped you,' she added teasingly.

He grinned and came to kiss her. 'Goodbye, Katerina. You're definitely my second favourite girl!'

Kate laughed and stood in the porch to wave to him as he turned out of the driveway and into the main road. She unlocked the door and carried the basket of groceries into the sitting-room. The shutters were closed and it was very dim in there. For a moment she couldn't see clearly, but then she stiffened as the sharp tang of tobacco smoke reached her. Hugo got lazily up from the chair where he had been lounging, ground out his cigarette, and walked calmly towards her.

'Come on in, Mrs Merrion,' he said menacingly. 'You and I have a lot to talk about.'

CHAPTER FIVE

KATE didn't stop to think, to wonder how on earth he had found out about the villa and been waiting for her. She threw the basket of groceries in his general direction and turned to run, a crazy idea that it still might not be too late to dash after Carlos and call him back running through her head. But Hugo was much too fast for her; dodging the basket and bridging the gap between them in one swift leap. With his left hand he pushed the door shut and with the other caught her by the shoulder and slammed her back against the wall, knocking the breath out of her.

'Oh, no, you don't,' he said grimly. 'You're not getting away from me again.'

He picked up the key from where she'd dropped it and locked the door, putting the key in his pocket. Then he stood over her, pinning her to the wall by her shoulders, his face, dark and angry, only a few inches away from her own. Kate stared back at him, her eyes wide with fright, her thoughts an incoherent jumble. He smiled unpleasantly when he saw the fear in her eyes.

'Yes, you're right to be afraid, because I've several scores to settle with you. But first you're going to do some talking.' Straightening up, he pulled her away from the wall and led her unresistingly across the room to push her down into the chair he had been sitting on. The upholstery was still warm from his body.

Kate stared at him as he hooked another chair forward to sit opposite her, just a couple of feet away. Taking his time, he lit a cigarette, watching her through the lighter flame. Wildly she looked around her, gripping the arms of the chair, ready to spring to her feet at the slightest chance of escape.

'Just try it,' Hugo's voice was even more dangerous because of its calmness, 'and you'll really have something to run away from.'

Slowly she sat back, realising that she wouldn't get more than two yards before he caught her and dragged her back. Desperately she looked into his face, hoping for some sign of pity or compassion, but his hard grey eyes were as cold as water over stone, his mouth set in an inflexible line. She was trapped like a fly in a spider's web, and she suddenly knew with utmost certainty that he wasn't going to hurry to seek his revenge. Now that he had her in his power he would take his time, exact every last ounce of retribution until he had completely humiliated and degraded her. And there was no one who could help her, no one who knew that she was alone with this man—a man who hated and despised her, and had sworn to make her pay for the supposed wrong she'd done him.

There was to be no help from outside, and perhaps because of it Kate found some strength within herself. All right, so he was mad at her, more furious than anyone she had ever seen, but that didn't mean he had the monopoly on anger; she had more right to be furious with him than he with her. It was his actions that had ruined their travesty of a marriage, not hers. She lifted her chin and faced him, defiance in her green eyes.

'You can ask all the questions you want, but I shan't

answer you. I don't know how you found me and I don't care. I just want to be free of you! So you can get out of here. I never want to see you again!' Her indignation had brought her to her feet, her voice hot with resentment, but it seemed to have no effect on Hugo at all.

'Sit down,' he said coldly. Only when she continued to defy him did he move. He reached up quite casually and put a hand on her neck, then slowly forced her down into the chair again. It was a silent struggle; Kate resisted him with all her strength, but he was so physically powerful that she knew he could even have forced her to her knees if he had wanted to. But he didn't, not yet; she had an idea that that final humiliation was still to come. He was breathing a little more heavily when he at last let her go, the glint in his eyes contemptuous. 'And now you know that I can force you to do anything I damn well want. So you'll sit there and you'll answer any question I put to you, do you understand?'

Huddled back in the chair, Kate could only nod in agreement. Her neck hurt abominably and there were tears of pain in the eyes she had turned away from him, but she was too proud to put her hand up to rub it, to let him see that he'd hurt her.

'All right. So who's Carlos? Is he the man who brought you here?'

'Yes. He's a—a friend.' She answered stiltedly, hating Hugo for forcing her to do so.

'A friend?' His tone was insulting. 'You mean a lover, don't you?'

Her head came round at that and she glared back at him. 'No, I don't! He's what I said—a friend.'

Hugo drew on his cigarette and looked at her disbelievingly, but he let it pass. 'How long have you known him?'

'Not long, just over a week.'

'Was that his house you were staying at in Palma?'

'Yes, he took me there because....' She broke off abruptly when she saw his lips curl in disdainful triumph.

'He picked you up, took you to his house, let you live with him, and you want me to believe he wasn't your lover?' His voice became brutal. 'You never had a platonic friendship in your life! I bet you delivered for every boy you dated, every man who gave you a good time. You little slut, I bet you even....'

'Stop it!' Kate had put her hands over her ears, unable to bear his vile accusations. 'That isn't true. None of it. I've never had a lover. I've never been to....'

His face black with rage, Hugo had risen sharply to his feet and pulled her up beside him, his hands on her arms, shaking her. 'You damn little liar! You're going to tell me the truth if it takes a month. And I don't care what I have to do to make you tell it.' He pushed her roughly back into the chair and stood towering over her. 'I want the truth and you're not leaving here until I get it.'

Kate stared up at him, her face bleak, trying to control the panic in her veins, knowing that he would refuse to believe anything but what he wanted to hear. As calmly as she could, she said, 'Hugo, please don't be like this. What's the point? There's nothing left between us, so why don't you just let me go instead of....'

'Instead of punishing you for what you did to me? Is that what you're trying to say?'

'Instead of punishing us both,' she said quietly, sadly.

Hugo laughed, a harsh, mirthless sound. 'Are you by any chance trying to appeal to my better nature, my dear Kate?' he asked sneeringly.

She bit her lip at his tone, but persevered. 'If you want to put it that way. You're a civilised man, Hugo. If you looked at it dispassionately you'd see that this—this episode between us is just a little thing, something that can soon be put behind us and forgotten,' she said earnestly. 'We can have the marriage quietly annulled so that we'll both be free to pick up our lives again.' She came to a halt as Hugo sat down again, pyramiding his fingers and listening to her with a sardonic curl to his mouth.

'Oh, please go on,' he said with mock politeness. 'In a moment you'll be persuading me that your walking out on me was for my own good.'

Looking away from him, Kate said painfully, 'Perhaps it was. Surely you must agree that it was better to find out that our relationship was founded on—on nothing but quicksand before we'd committed ourselves completely?' She got up and walked away from him towards the closed windows, leaning her head against the coolness of the glass.

He let her go, making no attempt to stop her, but his voice when he spoke cut like a scythe. 'Personally I should have thought the marriage service was a complete commitment.'

She swung round to face him then. 'But one that you had no intention of keeping. I heard you, Hugo! I heard you telling Adam Ralston about that detective you hired, about what you'd got lined up for me. Did you really think I'd have stayed after that?' she asked bitterly.

He got unhurriedly to his feet and came over to her. 'So you heard it all, did you?'

'Enough.'

'Enough to know that you'd never get what you wanted out of me; money, position—you know, all those things you saw in me that you fell in love with,' he said with brutal mockery. His hand came up under her chin, forcing her head up so that she had to look at him. 'No one plays me false and gets away with it, least of all someone I put my trust in. I said I'd make you pay and I meant it, and your walking out on me has only added to the account. There are only two things I want from you, and I intend to get them both before I kick you out of my life once and for all. And don't think you'll just be able to pick up your life where you left off. I've got money and I've got power, and I'm going to use them to make darn sure that no agency or publisher in Britain ever uses you again. You'll be finished at home for good.'

His voice had been fiercely angry, but now it changed and became almost savage, his fingers tightening on her chin. 'And don't think you can go running to the man you were living with for protection. He must have known that you were tricking me into marriage and connived at it, or why would he have let you go through with it, keeping well out of the way until you thought it was safe to meet him? I'm having enquiries made about him right now, and as soon as I find out who he is I'll ruin him, socially and financially!'

'No!' Kate stared at him appalled. To punish her was one thing, but to take his spite out on Leo was something she couldn't allow. 'No, please, Hugo, you don't understand. You mustn't hurt Leo.'

His jaw tightened. 'So I've got through to you at last, have I? Found something that really makes you afraid. Why? Is it because you're in love with him? Or because you're more afraid of what he might do to you than me? You had it all worked out nicely between you, didn't you? Set me up for the fall guy with your pretence of innocence and virginity so that you could milk me dry. Probably blackmail me into avoiding a scandal. While you and he would still be lovers in my marriage bed at every opportunity, I don't doubt,' he snarled at her. 'And when you overheard that I'd found out you did the next best thing. You bolted and then threatened a scandal unless I gave you an annulment and settled a small fortune on you in hush money.'

Vehemently Kate shook her head. 'That isn't true. I haven't asked you for a penny.'

'No?' Hugo asked ironically. 'In his letter your solicitor said that you were considerably out of pocket because of the wedding. Wouldn't you say that was paving the way for a settlement?'

Kate bit her lip unhappily. 'Simon must have put that to try to hurry things along. He knows I want to get back to work as soon as possible.'

'Simon? So you're on first name terms with your solicitor, are you?'

'He's a friend.'

'Another friend.' Hugo's tone was infinitely sarcastic, implying everything that was sordid. 'How convenient! You seem to have *friends* on hand wherever you need them.' His voice hardened. 'But it won't do you any good. None of your lovers can help you now, because

I'm going to break you, and I'm going to break Crawford, whoever he is.'

He let go of her abruptly and crossed to the table to pick up his cigarette. Noticing the groceries that had fallen out of the basket she'd thrown at him, he said peremptorily, 'Pick those things up, then you can cook something to eat,' adding sarcastically, 'Just think, darling, our first meal together as man and wife.'

Reluctantly Kate picked up the basket and began to put the things back into it. Her brain felt numb so she moved slowly, giving herself time to think. To try and make him see reason was impossible, and she knew that if she tried to tell him the truth, that Leo was her half-brother, he would just laugh in her face in utter disbelief. And she had no proof, nothing to back up her story. An orange had rolled behind a chair and she bent to retrieve it. Hugo had gone to the front door and was bringing in her cases. She edged towards the window, waiting until his back was turned while she pretended to concentrate on picking up pieces of fruit. When he went out for her third case she ran to the window and undid the catch. It was stiff and wouldn't open. Desperately she pushed at it, but it still wouldn't budge.

Hugo's hand came over hers, imprisoning it against the window frame. 'Didn't I tell you? I took the precaution of screwing the windows shut before you came. And the same goes for the shutters. You see, I didn't want anything to interfere with our honeymoon. Just you and I together in our villa on a sun-soaked island. Romantic, isn't it?' he said with contemptuous mockery.

Kate found that she couldn't look at him. She stared instead at his hand, long-fingered and strong, completely covering her own.

Abruptly he let her go free. 'Now finish what you were doing,' he ordered.

Slowly she obeyed him, carrying the basket of groceries into the kitchen and putting it on the table.

'There are some steaks in the fridge,' he told her. 'Cook those with a side salad.'

Her head came up resentfully at his tone, but his grey eyes stared back at her, daring her to defy him. At length she lowered her head and began to prepare the meal.

The unexpected turn of events had left her feeling totally confused. How on earth had he known about the villa? And more important still, how was she going to get away from him? Trying to reason with him had been a complete waste of time, so her only hope was to escape from the villa as soon as she could. Because she had no illusions about what would happen if she didn't. Hugo had only married her because he wanted to possess her sexually, and she had no doubt that now he had her in his power he wouldn't hesitate to take her, coldly and ruthlessly. And she somehow thought that the more she struggled and fought him off, the more satisfaction he would get out of it.

As she worked she tried to think of a plan, to decide on some course of action. He had said that he had screwed down the windows and shutters and she had seen him lock the front door, so that left only the door leading out from the kitchen to the courtyard and the pool. Admittedly there was a six-foot-high wall all round the courtyard, but she could always stand on something and climb over. Or if she could reach the windmill tower she could easily go up the outside steps and jump into the field beyond. But first she would have to try and lull Hugo into thinking she was cowed and docile. At the moment he was watching her like a hawk, sitting casually at the table but his eyes never leaving her, ready to spring up if she tried anything. So she finished the salad and carried it and the steaks to the table where she sat down opposite him.

He took a bottle of wine from the rack and uncorked it, pouring the blood-red liquid into two glasses. He lifted his and looked at her over the rim. 'To us,' he said sardonically.

Kate ignored this and they ate in a heavy, tense silence. When she had finished Kate picked up her glass but didn't drink, instead swirling the remainder of the wine round, watching it absorbedly. 'How *did* you find me?' she asked him.

He looked at her frowningly for a moment as if making up his mind, then shrugged. 'It was simple. As soon as I found you'd bolted from the reception I got in touch with the detective agency again and told them to find you. When they checked with the airport passenger lists they discovered that you'd flown to Majorca, and one of the ground staff remembered you from a photograph. One advantage of looking for someone with a face like yours is that you're easy to find. He remembered that a man had brought you and had given you money. The agency had connections with a similar set-up in Palma, so I instructed them to send people to every likely place you might go. The man who saw you in the town followed you to your car and then on here.' He smiled maliciously when he saw the look of chagrin that came to her face. 'I had some covering up to do in England first, but I came as soon as I knew you were definitely here and seemed likely to stay. But when I got to the villa you'd gone and so had all your belongings. For a while I thought you'd tricked me again, but then I had a stroke of luck. I hung around the town where you'd first been seen and saw you driving through with your latest lover.' He said the word deliberately, enjoying the flush that came to her cheeks.

'I had the car number traced and set someone to watch his house, in the meantime getting this place ready in case you came back here. Tell me,' he added malevolently, 'does he know you're married? Or are you stringing him along in the hope that I'll give you a quick annulment so that you can really get your hooks into him?' He raised an eyebrow. 'Maybe you were telling the truth at that. The report I've had on him tells me he's a bachelor, and rich, very rich. In which case you've probably played the same game with him, told him the same lies as you told me. Is that it, Kate? Does he think you're a pure, innocent virgin? While all the time you're just a conniving, shameless little slut who doesn't give a damn who she hurts so long as she....'

'Shut up!' Kate came to her feet, realised that the glass of wine was still in her hand and went to throw it in his face. But he was expecting it and his hand came up and caught her wrist, forcing her arm down until she set the glass on the table again.

'So I've guessed that ploy too, have I? Why did he send you back here? Did he see through your game and kick you out, or was there some other reason?'

He was still pinioning her wrist against the table. Unsteadily Kate said, 'I wasn't playing any game. His mother thought ... she asked me to....' She broke off unhappily, her voice sounding unconvincing even to her own ears.

'So his mother saw through you and got rid of you, did she?' he asked jeeringly. 'What a shame, Kate,' he went on with mock sympathy. 'You just don't seem to be having much luck at getting your dirty little hands on some man's money lately, do you? What about your lover, Crawford? Can't he afford you any longer?' His voice sharpened. 'Or is he the one who's put you up to all this? Is it for him that you're trying to get hold of a rich husband?' He stared at her, eyes narrowed. 'My God, you must really love him,' he said softly.

Kate's head came up and her eyes met his. 'More than you'll ever know,' she said defiantly.

The look in his eyes became almost murderous and for a moment she thought she had gone too far. His grip on her wrist tightened forcibly and she gave an involuntary wince of pain. His mouth twisted in cruel satisfaction. Then his face changed; he altered his grip and with his other hand reached up to pull back her sleeve to reveal the crêpe bandage, the thickness of which he'd felt through her shirt.

'What have you done to it?'

'It's nothing.'

She tried to pull her hand away, but he wouldn't let go, instead unpinning the bandage and starting to unwind it. 'I asked you what you'd done to it,' he repeated grimly as he took off the bandage and saw the welt of bruising that was starting to turn from red to a livid black-blue.

'I was kicked by a horse,' she answered tonelessly. It seemed so long ago, yet if it hadn't happened she wouldn't have left the villa and Hugo would have found her a week ago.

'I didn't know you could ride.'

'I can't. I got in the way, that's all.'

'And these other marks?' He pointed to four smaller, still red bruises on top of the others.

Her hand began to shake in his and he looked up sharply. 'They're nothing. They don't matter.' Despite a brave effort to control it, her voice was unsteady.

'Those are finger marks. Who made them? Answer me!'

'All right!' She tore her hand from his grasp. 'If you really want to know, you did. When you tried to drag me out of the club last night.' She pushed her hair back out of her eyes with shaking fingers. 'So that's something else for you to gloat over, isn't it? Something else for your rotten vindictive ego to feed on. Any other man would have realised that he'd made a mistake and just walked away from this.' Her voice rose wildly. 'But not you! Oh, no, you have to send your spies out to track me down, and then you lock me up in here with you, determined to frighten and punish me. Tell me, what did you do for kicks before you had me to push around?'

Hugo had also risen to his feet, his face taut with anger as she yelled at him, but now he stepped swiftly round the table and came towards her. 'Shut up, you're becoming hysterical. If you don't stop it I'll have to hit you.'

Kate laughed in his face. 'Don't tell me you need an excuse,' she jeered.

His hands reached out and caught her shoulders, there was a tense look about his face as if he was having difficulty in controlling himself. 'Damn you, shut up! Do you think I would have hurt you again if I'd known your wrist was already injured?'

'Yes, I think you would. I think you'd do almost any-thing to hurt me,' she said bitterly. 'You're inhuman. An animal!'

'Oh, no, don't drag me down to your level,' Hugo said in something like a snarl. 'You're the lying, cheat-ing little rat, remember? I'm not going to force you to do anything.'

She had been vainly trying to push his hands away, but now she stood still, staring up at him, her hair dishevelled and her eyes wide with surprise. 'Then what the hell are you doing here?'

His mouth twisted sardonically as he saw the sudden gleam of hope in her amber-flecked eyes. 'Oh, don't worry, I fully intend to get what I came for.' His hand moved along to slip inside her shirt and caress her throat. 'But even though the idea is certainly very tempting, I don't intend to use force on you. No, by the time I've finished with you you'll give me the two things I want: the complete truth about your past and,' he paused as he deliberately let his eyes run over her, his fingers hot against her skin, 'and your extremely desir-able body, quite willingly. It may take time, of course, but then I have plenty of time, thanks to that long, romantic honeymoon we planned.'

Too appalled to speak, Kate could only stare into the hard grey eyes, filled with cruel mockery. So now she knew! He wouldn't lower himself to use brute force— oh no, that would be much too uncivilised for the suave Hugo Merrion. Instead he intended to keep on and on at her, wear her down with his questions and accusations until she was ready to confess to anything just to be free of him. But not only confess; he also wanted the final and utmost degradation—to coldbloodedly give herself to him. But that he should never have. Whatever else he might torment her into doing he could never make her do that. And the certainty of the thought gave her courage.

She let out her breath on a long, shuddering sigh and said coldly, 'Take your hands off me.'

He gave a thin smile. 'As your husband, I've a perfect right to handle you any time I want.'

Kate's voice was quite steady. 'No, you haven't. You forfeited any rights you ever had over me when you set that detective to watch me.' Then she slipped from his suddenly slack grasp and walked away from him into the living-room.

He came after her at once. 'Just what was that supposed to mean?'

Turning, Kate faced him squarely. 'You're so damn sure of yourself, aren't you? Did it ever occur to you that you might have made a mistake? You read that detective's report and immediately believed every word of it, not even giving me the opportunity to admit or deny anything it said. You had so little trust in me that you didn't hesitate to condemn me. But perhaps that was because your own actions had been so false. You were ready to believe the worst of me because you were a liar yourself. Well, I'll tell you something, Hugo: I never lied to you, not once. But I'm glad that you believed that report, because it showed me what you were really like, what I'd been too blind and besotted to see.'

'You'll be telling me next that you were really in love with me,' Hugo broke in derisively. 'Nice try, Kate, but you don't seriously expect me to believe it?'

She looked at him for a moment, then turned away. 'No. No, I don't,' she said tiredly.

'Especially when you've already told me that you're in love with this man Crawford.'

'I didn't say I was in love with him, only that I loved him.'

'There's a difference?'

'Yes, a great difference.'

He looked at her consideringly. 'Of course there is always one way for you to prove you're speaking the truth.' His voice had suddenly changed, become smooth as silk.

Swinging her head round, Kate gazed at him in surprise. 'There is? How?'

His mouth twisted into a thin smile. 'By coming to bed with me and letting me find out for myself if you're still a virgin.'

Her breath coming out in an incredulous gasp, Kate said unsteadily, 'Why, you—you sadist! I'll never give myself to you! I'd rather....'

'Kill yourself first?' he asked sarcastically. 'Oh, come now, don't be so melodramatic. You know you....'

'No!' she interrupted passionately. 'I'd rather kill *you* first!'

For a moment they stared at each other, then Hugo said slowly, 'We shall just have to find out, then, won't we? Because I'm definitely going to....'

The telephone rang shrilly, cutting off his words. Hugo reacted first but had to look round for the phone, whereas Kate had the advantage of knowing exactly where it was. Diving across the room, she snatched off the receiver.

'Carlos, that man from the club is holding me prisoner! You've got to help me.'

The last few words were shouted desperately as Hugo came behind her and wrenched the receiver from her grasp. He pulled her back against him and put his forearm hard against her throat, almost choking her, so that she couldn't cry out or struggle.

'Hallo, who is that?' His voice sounded only slightly breathless as he spoke into the receiver. His mouth twisted into a smile as he listened, then said, 'No, it was just a child playing a joke. Yes, I'll take a call from England.'

Kate went limp with chagrin as she realised she'd only spoken to the operator, but then Hugo was speaking again.

'Simon? Oh, you must be Kate's solicitor. This is Hugo Merrion.' A choking sound came from Kate's lips as she tried to call for help, but Hugo tightened his muscles and she could only make unintelligible noises. 'Yes, I expect it is a surprise,' he was answering Simon. 'But as it happens Kate and I have got together again. It was all a rather terrible mistake, as Kate would have found out if she hadn't run off like that. Naturally I followed her and explained everything as soon as I caught up with her. Yes, everything's fine now, thanks, Kate won't be needing your services after all.' Kate glared at him, her body paralysed within his hold, her eyes full of enmity, but he merely raised his eyebrows in amusement as he went on talking. 'We've decided to have our honeymoon here instead. Have the villa as long as we like?' He frowned, then recovered quickly. 'Thanks, we're grateful. No, I'm sorry I can't put Kate on to talk to you at the moment, she's taking a shower, but I'll tell her you called.' Then his voice hardened. 'Leo Crawford? Yes, as you say, she should have told me about him long ago. Goodbye.' He gently replaced the receiver but didn't let her go straight away.

'So even your solicitor knows about your lover, does he? And this place belongs to him and not your Spanish boy-friend. On the whole quite a fruitful and interesting phone call, which leaves you with quite a lot of explaining to do.'

He let her go abruptly and Kate put her hands up to rub her neck. 'I thought you weren't going to use force,' she said croakily.

'Not to make you do what I want; keeping you here until I get it is a different matter. And that wasn't force, merely a trick they taught me in the army.' He looked at her frowningly. 'You weren't expecting a call from your solicitor, you used the name Carlos first of all. Are you expecting a call from him too?'

'You'll just have to wait and see, won't you?' Kate answered in a proud but pitiful attempt at defiance. Pitiful because she knew that Carlos was hardly likely to phone her when the family would be celebrating his engagement to Consuelo. Obviously he had told Simon where she was and to phone her direct rather than relay a message. In fact Carlos probably wouldn't give her another thought until he called to collect her and take her to the airport. And that wouldn't be for another two days. Two days of being shut up here alone with Hugo! She grinned mirthlessly to herself; less than a month ago that would have seemed like the peak of happiness, but now.... Lord, it was almost funny in its irony.

Hugo had been watching the play of expressions on

her face. 'What are you trying to hide?'

She shrugged. 'Nothing. I was just thinking how very grotesque life can be.'

'Don't tell me you're starting to have twinges of conscience?' he said derisively. 'That's about as believable as all the other lies you've tried to spin me. Why don't you face it, Kate? No one's going to help you. I've got you here and I'm going to keep you, and the sooner you make up your mind to that and give me what I want, the sooner you'll be free.'

'Free?' Kate lifted her head to gaze at him. 'If I told you all you wanted to know, you'd let me go?'

'That isn't all I want and you know it.'

'If I gave you that too, then, tonight. You'd leave here? I'd never have to see you again?'

'I've already said so.' He was very still, very tense, his eyes watching her closely.

For a few minutes she returned his gaze, then slowly shook her head. 'Oh, no, you wouldn't let me go that easily. You wouldn't get enough satisfaction out of such an easy victory. You'd still keep me here to squeeze as much sadistic pleasure as you could out of crushing me. You won't be satisfied until I beg you to let me go. Well, I won't, not ever!' She was standing very stiffly, chin raised in obstinate challenge. 'Because I've done nothing to be ashamed of, and there's nothing you can do to hurt me, not any more. The only person you're hurting is yourself, with this crazy, insane insistence on. . . .'

'That's where you're wrong.' Hugo took a decisive step towards her and Kate hurriedly backed away, to be brought up short by a chair. Almost casually he reached out and pushed her into it, putting his hands on the arms and leaning down to loom menacingly over her. 'You may be hard as nails under that beautiful exterior, but you're nowhere near tough enough to withstand me. That arm-lock wasn't the only trick I learned in the army; they taught me several pleasant little ways to make reluctant people talk—oh, nothing physical, just nice, gentle persuasion, that goes on and on and on. And don't think I'll make it any easier because you're a woman. You'll get on your hands and knees and crawl to me before I'm through with you, my lovely, cheating wife!'

Kate stared at him in stunned dismay as he sat in a chair opposite hers, deliberately lit himself a cigarette, then leaned forward to switch on a lamp and turn it to shine directly in her face.

'All right, let's start. How long has this man Crawford been your lover?'

'You're crazy. Do you really think you can get away with this third degree stuff?'

'How long has Crawford been your lover?' he repeated, completely ignoring her outburst.

'Go to hell! I'm not going to tell you anything.'

But he kept on repeating the same question over and over again, until she covered up her ears to cut out the sound of his voice. He dragged her hands down and started again, varying the questions now but always with the same basis. 'How long have you known him? Where is he now? Why does he need money? When did he put you up to marrying me? How long have you lived with him?'

At first she yelled back at him, tried to drown his voice, but as the room grew darker, with only the bright light of the lamp glaring in her eyes, she could no

longer see him, and his voice, keeping relentlessly on
and on, became almost a disembodied thing, like a
record that had got stuck in the same groove, forever
repeating itself. She didn't know how long it went on
for, it seemed like hours, and he didn't give up until
she'd taken refuge in the only weapon she had—
complete silence. She tried to cut his voice out completely, but it was impossible to ignore it, it was so
insistent. She felt utterly exhausted, her brain numb
from his continuous probing. Only after she'd been
completely quiet for a long while did he stop and turn
off the lamp. The sudden darkness almost frightened
her and she gave a little gasp of alarm.

'It's all right, Kate. It's all over now.' His voice had
suddenly became strangely gentle. It didn't seem to
belong to that hateful person who had questioned her
at all. He stood up and drew her to her feet, catching
her when she staggered from having been made to sit
still for so long. The warmth of his arms seemed a
haven of safety and strength. Leaning her head against
his chest, she clung to him weakly as he stroked her
hair. 'There, there.' He comforted her like a child.
'You were very good. You didn't tell about Leo, did
you? Although you could easily have told me that
you've known him for five years.'

Kate could still see the bright glow of the lamp in
her face, there were blinding flashes of light still in her
eyes, and she felt dizzy and disorientated, her brain
whirling, aware only of the blessed relief that it was
all over. 'No, not five years,' she mumbled. 'Known him
all my life.' Her head throbbed and ached. She sagged
against this person who was being kind to her.

'And you've lived with him a long time, haven't

you?' It was hardly more than a whisper in her ear.

'Mm. Ever since—ever since I came to London.' She felt so sleepy, so exhausted. She closed her eyes, but that made the flashes worse.

'Where is he now?'

'Gone. Gone Argentina.'

'You'll miss him, won't you? You'll miss your lover, won't you, Kate?'

Perhaps it was the tension in his body, perhaps a slight harshness Hugo was unable to keep out of his voice, no matter how he tried, that gave some warning to her dulled brain. She became suddenly rigid under his hands, aware of where she was and who was holding her. With one convulsive movement she broke free of him and stood staring at him wildly, like a frightened creature at bay.

'Oh, my God! You're despicable. Of all the lowdown, dirty tricks!' She ran to the side of the room and turned on the light. Hugo stood facing her, hands in his pockets, apparently quite unperturbed, only a slight twist to his mouth betraying his annoyance that his ruse hadn't worked completely.

'Next time,' he threatened softly. 'Or the one after that. There'll be plenty more next times, you beautiful little bitch.'

CHAPTER SIX

It was stiflingly hot in the airless room. Kate lay on the bed with only a thin nightdress on, the covers thrown back. She moved restlessly, head still aching and unable to sleep, her mind constantly going over and over the predicament in which she found herself, forever seeking some way of escape. Because she couldn't face another session like tonight's, she just knew she couldn't.

After she had refused to answer his questions, Hugo had let her unpack some of her clothes and then take a shower. Deliberately she had locked the bathroom door, but after she had been in there for only about a quarter of an hour, he had banged on the door and told her to come out. For a crazy moment she had thought of defying him, but rejected the idea almost at once. It wouldn't take him two minutes to kick the door open and there was no way she wanted to arouse his anger at this time of night when she was wearing only her bathrobe. So she had opened the door and come out, hair brushed loose and falling to her shoulders, her hand clutching at the neck of the robe and pulling it closer around her.

Hugo was waiting outside, leaning apparently negligently against the wall. His eyes ran over her appraisingly and she instinctively shrank back.

His mouth twisted sardonically. 'You don't have to be afraid, I've never forced myself on a woman yet and

I don't intend to start with a little tramp like you. Unless you push me so far that I forget myself, that is,' he added threateningly. 'You can have this room.' He led her to the second bedroom and held open the door. 'As you can see, the windows and shutters have been fastened down here too. And don't get any ideas about trying to sneak out during the night, because I'll be sleeping in the main bedroom and you'd have to go past it to get to the kitchen. And I'm a very light sleeper.' There was a distinct hint of menace in his voice.

Kate looked at him antagonistically. 'All right, you don't have to spell it out. I've got the message. If I step out of line you'll forget all your noble pretensions not to use force, is that it?'

'You're learning fast.' He strolled over to the dressing-table and picked up her make-up bag, upending it to let the contents fall out with a clatter. 'I'll just take these in case you try to unscrew the window.' He sorted out a nail file and a pair of scissors from her manicure case. 'Sleep well—if you can.'

She'd shut the door behind him immediately he'd gone, but there was no lock on it. After a while she heard the sound of running water and she had the sudden thought that she might be able to slip past while he was under the shower. Gingerly she opened the door a fraction and looked out. He had the bathroom door wide open to give him a good view of the corridor. Hastily she pushed her door shut again. Slowly she got ready for bed, putting on a cotton nightdress. Already the air in the room was warm and close with nothing to disturb it and create a breeze. There was an electric fan in the sitting-room, but she knew without even thinking about it that he wouldn't let her have it; no concessions to the enemy in this battle of wits he was determined to wage against her.

Now Kate lay on the bed, still awake, hot and sticky with perspiration, her throat dry and parched. She longed for a drink of water, but was afraid to go to the bathroom to get one in case Hugo might wake and put the wrong interpretation on it. It seemed as if she had lain here for hours, racking her brain to find some means of either getting away or of persuading him to let her go. But she could think of nothing that would be even half way effective in either case. Her one hope that she kept coming back to was that Carlos was coming for her in two days—no, it would be the day after tomorrow now, she realised as she looked at her watch and saw that it was two in the morning. And once Carlos came Hugo would have no choice but to let her go. She could threaten him with the police if he didn't. With Carlos to protect her she would be safe. But first she would have to get through the long hours of waiting, hours in which she would have to keep all her wits about her if she was to resist Hugo's brain-washing methods.

She turned on the pillow and a sharp stab of pain shot through her head just between her eyes. Damn Hugo, she couldn't stand this any longer. Swinging her legs out of bed, she groped for her negligee and pulled it on, then padded over to the door. He had left the light on in the corridor. She went into the bathroom, shutting the door but not locking it. She found the cord for the razor light over the mirror and pulled it down. For a few seconds she was dazzled. She blinked and found herself staring into the mirror. The face that stared back at her was flushed with heat, but there were dark, smudgy circles about her tired eyes and a curious white tautness around her mouth. Kate gazed at her reflection for a moment and then deliberately pushed the mirror to one side to search in the medicine cabinet that lay behind it for some aspirins. Eventually she found a bottle with 'Aspirins' penned on it in English over the Spanish brand name. She filled a glass with water and shook a couple of the tablets into her hand.

'What are you doing? Give me those!' Hugo's voice was harsh behind her as he spun her away from the basin and grabbed the bottle from her hand. 'What the hell are you trying to do?' He was wearing just pyjama trousers, his chest bronzed and powerful.

'Oh, for heaven's sake! I have a headache. I came in here to take some aspirins. I should think I'm damn well entitled to have a headache after what you put me through tonight, added to which I'm almost stifling in that little room without any fresh air. Look, two aspirins, that's all.' She held them up in her fingers to show him. 'Did you really think I'd be stupid enough to try to kill myself because of you? No way!' she said jeeringly. 'You're not worth it, no matter how much you hurt me.' She picked up the glass and swallowed the pills, then deliberately turned her back on him to soak a clean face flannel in cold water and bathe her burning forehead. With her eyes half closed, she lifted her head to run the cool cloth over her face and neck. When she opened them again she found that Hugo was watching her in the mirror, a curious expression on his face that she couldn't fathom. When he caught her eyes on him he quickly looked away.

'Finished?'

She nodded.

He watched her go back to her room. 'Leave the door open, you'll get more air.' Silently she obeyed him.

It took time for the aspirins to work and as Kate lay there she remembered a modelling job she had once done to advertise a brand of aspirin that was supposed to give instant relief. She could have done with some of those now—and the manufacturers had given her a free giant-sized jar too. She turned restlessly. If only she had some air! It would be better to sleep in the bathroom than this room that felt more like a sauna every minute; at least it had been cooler there. Kate wasn't quite sure when she realised why it had been cooler. But of course, the window in the bathroom had a metal frame and he hadn't been able to screw it down, and it had no shutters behind it! It must have been open just enough to let in a flow of fresh air.

Feverishly she sat up in bed, trying to remember exactly how big the window was, or rather how small, because she seemed to recall that it was more like a fanlight set high into the wall overlooking the courtyard. Was it big enough for her to get through? Was it? As quietly as she could she crept to the open door and looked across at the bathroom, straining to see the window. Darn, she couldn't see without actually going inside. The window was terribly small, only about eighteen inches by twelve, but it would have to do. Quickly she hurried back to her room. If Hugo had heard anything he must have thought she was getting another drink, because he didn't come to see what she was doing.

Kate gave a sigh of relief and began silently to change into a tee-shirt and figure hugging jeans; she couldn't afford to wear anything loose that might catch, and she pushed her feet into a pair of soft-soled tennis shoes. Her money and passport were still in her hand-bag in the sitting-room but they were the least of her worries, getting away was all that mattered now.

Stealthily she crept out into the corridor again. The bed creaked in Hugo's room and she stood as though turned to stone, her heart pumping with fright. But there were no further sounds, all was still. Kate gulped and forced herself to go on. After all, he couldn't eat her, could he? No, but he can do something almost as unpleasant, and he will if I push him too far, whispered a small, frightened voice inside her. Once inside the bathroom, she turned the key in the lock but didn't dare turn on the light. Luckily there was moonlight shining through the window, thrown into grotesque patterns by the mottled glass. Slowly she climbed on to the loo seat and then inch by inch eased the window open. Stretching up, she got one leg through and then the other, the catch digging into her flesh as she twisted to get her hips through. Stifling a yelp of pain, she went on wriggling through the narrow gap. For a horrible moment she thought that her shoulders were going to get stuck, but then the sheer weight of the rest of her body pulled her through, although she felt as if a lump of her right shoulder had been gouged out by the catch. For a second she hung by her hands, then let herself drop the few inches to the ground.

Without pausing for a moment she ran across the courtyard past the pool, her feet making little noise on the tiled surround. The windmill sails were still, locked in place so that they couldn't turn, but even if they had been free they wouldn't have turned tonight. The air was humid and still, only a few clouds blotting the clear sky turned almost into day by the brilliance of the full moon. As quickly as she could, Kate ran up the outside staircase of the tower, keeping close to the wall because the narrow stone steps were worn with age and weather and there was no rail to hold on to. The other side of the tower formed part of the boundary wall and there were olive and almond trees growing close up against it on the outside.

Breathless, Kate paused as she looked down. She would have to be careful where she jumped; she didn't want to impale herself on a branch. Then she became aware that what she had thought to be the deep, dark shadow of the trees wasn't a shadow at all. It was the roof of a black car that had been parked close up against the wall. But why on earth ... ? Then it penetrated. Of course, that was how Hugo must have got into the villa, by climbing on the roof of the car and then on to the stairway, and once inside the courtyard it would have been a relatively easy task for him to force a window and get inside the house. And he would have left the car here, out of sight of the road so that she would have no warning that he was there, waiting for her to step into his trap.

Kate gave a grim smile. Well, it would come in very handy for something he hadn't reckoned on; to help her without the risk of breaking an ankle. She jumped lightly down, the roof making a protesting, metallic sound as she landed on it. Crouching down, she kept very still, afraid that he might have heard the noise, for sounds carried a long way at night. The noise of crickets was all around her as they jumped through the long grass. Kate had seen them before; they were huge

things, over an inch long with black shiny bodies. She
shivered, an inherent fear of insects making her afraid
of the beastly things that could jump from yards away
to land at your feet.

But now was no time to worry about crickets! As
quietly as she could she transferred her weight to the
bonnet of the car and this time the metal didn't make
a noise, thank goodness. From there she vaulted lightly
to the ground, running through the small grove and
then standing at the edge to look back at the villa. It
was still in darkness—she was safe.

For a moment she toyed with the idea of running
down the driveway to the road and then to the village.
But that was a couple of miles away. Hugo might wake
and find her gone, come after her in the car and catch
her. No, the nearest place of safety would be the best,
and that was the neighbouring farm where the farmer
had sold her the vegetables. It was going to be hell trying to explain in Spanish, but she would have had to
do that anyway if she went to the village. At least the
farmer knew who she was.

Quickly she started to run across the field, not making
as much progress as she would have liked because of
the uneven ground. Her breath came in quick pants,
tiredness and fatigue slowing her down when she
needed her strength most, but the knowledge of what
lay behind her kept her going on. She came to the first
stone wall and scrambled over it. Only two more fields
and she would be there, but how much bigger the fields
were than they had looked from the villa. Panting, she
glanced up at the farmhouse, but even as she did so a
cloud moved slowly but inexorably in front of the
moon, plunging everything into sudden pitch darkness.

Darn! But she couldn't risk waiting for it to come out again. Any moment Hugo might find out that she'd gone. She had to keep going.

Trying to keep in the direction of the farm, she ran on, surprisingly making better time because this field was grassed and not planted with crops. Thankfully she lengthened her stride. Suddenly there was a movement straight in front of her as a black object seemed to rise up out of the ground towards her. Kate gave a cry of fright and then fell flat on her face, her legs and feet tangled up with something alive, something hard and yet soft. The thing was struggling to free itself almost as frantically as she was, and as it did so a bell began to ring like a gong through the night as the animal started to bray with fright.

Oh, hell! She'd fallen over a sheep!

Immediately every other stupid animal in the field started to join in the chorus as if they were in peril of their lives, running around and cannoning into one another in the darkness until it sounded as if all hell was let loose. For several minutes Kate was too petrified to move, and when she tried to get to her feet one of the sheep came running against her and knocked her down again. It was too dark to see and she'd lost her sense of direction, but then, thankfully, the blessed moon came out again and she picked herself up to run with frantic haste towards the farmhouse. The din must have wakened Hugo, but it must also have wakened the farmer and his family. She only had to get to the farm and they would be there ready to help her.

The sheep were dashing out of the way as she ran through them and a light had appeared in one of the windows of the farm. The sight gave her added strength and she staggered hopefully on, her breath coming in ragged pants.

She didn't hear him come up behind her, heard nothing but her own gasping breath, and had no idea that he was there until Hugo sent her flying to the ground to land face down in the dust of the field. He was beside her in a moment, his knee in the small of her back, pulling her arms behind her to hold them in a grip that was like a vice. His other hand came round to cover her mouth so that she couldn't scream, and then he was dragging her to her feet and half-carrying her back towards the villa. The elements were on his side, even as she heard the farmhouse door open the moon again went behind a cloud.

Hugo got her to the wall easily, but as he climbed over he had to change his grip a little. With a desperate shove Kate broke free, but only for a second; she got to the other side of the wall and then fell as he managed to trip her. Landing on her side, Kate turned to claw at him as he reached for her. As she kicked out at him he fell on top of her, his hands trying to clutch her flailing wrists. They rolled together in the dirt, Hugo's breath coming in uneven, panting gasps after his headlong run to catch her. He was having a hard time trying to hold her as her body bucked and heaved under his.

'Damn you, keep still!' he snarled.

Kate felt her nails gouge furrows down his arm. She fought wildly, trying to get her legs free to knee him, but he was lying completely on top of her now, holding her down by his weight. Her struggles were becoming weaker as the last of her strength was spent and he managed to catch her wrists. Desperately she opened her mouth to scream.

Hugo hadn't had time to grip both her wrists in one hand, so he did the only thing he could to stop her. His mouth closed over hers, effectively silencing her. Rolling her head from side to side in the dust of the field, Kate vainly tried to break loose. She could feel the anger and determination behind the brutality of his embrace. With her teeth she found his lip and tried to bite him, but he forced her lips apart, pressing her head back into the ground. The knowledge that it was useless to go on fighting hit her suddenly and with it came extreme exhaustion. Their struggles had been hidden from the farmer by the wall; there was no one to help her, she'd failed completely.

She went limp under him, no longer offering any resistance, expecting him to get up and drag her back to the villa. But he didn't get up. He went on kissing her with raging insistence, his lips hard as they explored her mouth, not caring whether or not she responded. His breathing was ragged and uneven, his body in just the thin pyjamas hard against her own. God, did he mean to ...? The danger she was in gave her a last burst of frantic strength. She jerked her head to one side long enough to say sharply, 'No! No, Hugo, please!'

The fear in her cry got through to him. He became very still and she could feel his heart hammering in his chest so close to her own. At last he rolled off her and sat up slowly, staring at her, his eyes glazed. Kate was too frightened to move, her breath coming in little terrified sobs. He ran a dusty hand through his hair, then stood up, pulling her with him. Silently he took hold of her arm and she walked stumblingly beside him back to the house.

Once inside he took her back to her room and pushed her down on the bed.

'How the hell did you get out?' He was still slightly out of breath, but the glazed look had left his eyes and he was completely in control of himself again.

For a moment Kate didn't answer as she tried to think of some means of keeping her way of escape to herself in the hope of using it again.

'Answer me. How did you get out?' He sat on the edge of the bed and pushed her back against the pillow. 'If you don't tell me I shall have no alternative but to tie you to the bed,' he threatened grimly.

Kate had an idea. She pretended to glare at him morosely. 'All right, if you must know I went out through the kitchen door.'

'You little liar. You couldn't possibly have done. The door was locked, I made sure of that.'

'I daresay you did, but there just happens to be a duplicate key that's always kept handy.'

'Where?' he asked sharply.

But Kate was ready for that one. 'In the cutlery drawer, if you must know.'

'And just how did you get past me?'

'I crawled across the floor. You were lying on your back, snoring,' she added nastily.

'Was I indeed?' There was a brief flash of something like wry amusement in the hard eyes that glared down at her. 'And where is the duplicate key now?'

'In my pocket. I put it there after I relocked the door. I suppose you want it.' She rolled on to her side and pretended to feel in the back pocket of her jeans. 'It's gone. It must have fallen out when you were demonstrating some more of your unpleasant unarmed combat tricks.' She glanced quickly up at him under her lashes, wondering if he had fallen for her ruse, but he wasn't watching her; instead he seemed more interested in her shoulder.

'How did you do this?' His finger was following a jagged tear in her tee-shirt.

'What?' Kate squinted over her shoulder at the tear and her heart began to beat loudly as she realised she must have done it when she'd got stuck in the window. She shrugged. 'During that fight in the field, I suppose,' she said as offhandedly as she could.

'I wonder.' Without warning he caught hold of her shirt and began to pull it over her head. She hardly had time to even begin to resist before he'd pulled it off and turned her on to her face. Grimly he examined the red marks on her shoulders. 'You didn't get those in any struggle. You've rubbed against something sharp.' He turned her over again none too gently. 'So we'll start again, shall we? And this time you'll tell me the truth or I might just start again where I left off in the field. Now, how did you get out?'

His arms were across her, pinning her down, his face menacingly close. Kate turned her head away so that she didn't have to look at him. 'Through the bathroom window,' she said dully.

He gave a surprised exclamation, then got up and went to look. She heard him moving about and then the sound of hammering from outside. Which meant, she supposed, that there wouldn't be another chance of escaping that way. Dejectedly she sat on the edge of the bed, her clothes and hair dirty, and feeling completely exhausted. At length Hugo came back and leaned against the door jamb, looking at her derisively.

'I've put a wire mesh over the window. I hadn't realised you were thin enough to get through such a narrow gap. Silly of me, I should have remembered that any woman who earns her living as a glorified coat-hanger has to be skinny.'

Kate could have retorted that he'd found her figure more than adequate once, but she decided to ignore him. 'I want to have a shower, I'm dirty.'

'You're that all right,' he replied, not meaning her appearance at all. 'But you'll just have to wait till the morning. I've lost enough sleep because of you already.'

'But I can't go back to bed like this,' she protested. 'My hair's full of dirt and dust.'

'Too bad. You should have thought of that before you tried to be a nocturnal Bo-peep.'

He went away, and Kate slowly stripped off her jeans and underclothes. She brushed as much of the dirt out of her hair as she could, but it still felt gritty and horrid. Wearily she put her nightdress back on and climbed into bed. At least it was cooler now that the night was nearly over and dawn on the way. Too tired even to worry, she turned on to her side and slept.

It was daylight when she awoke although the room was still in semi-darkness because of the closed shutters. For a moment she thought she was still in Carlos' house, but then she saw her torn tee-shirt lying on the floor where Hugo had thrown it and memory came back like a flood. Reaching out for her watch, she found that it was almost ten-thirty. She gave a little groan as she stretched, her shoulders felt stiff and sore. Would she be able to have a shower now? she wondered. Carefully she stepped into the corridor and looked into Hugo's room expecting to see him still asleep, but the place was empty, the shutters and windows wide open and letting in the streaming sunlight and wonderful fresh air.

At first she was taken aback, but then realised that the window of his room overlooked the courtyard and there was no danger of her trying to get out that way again because Hugo was already out there swimming strongly up and down the pool. But if he was in the pool he wouldn't be able to see what she was doing in the house. Quickly she ran into the sitting-room. The door was locked, of course, but there was still the phone. But Hugo had forestalled her; the table where it had stood was empty, the wire disconnected from the wall socket. And when she went into the kitchen to look for something to unscrew a window she found that he'd taken the cutlery drawer outside by the pool where he could see it.

Exasperatedly she stared out at him; the water looked crystal-cool and infinitely inviting. Well, why not? she thought rebelliously. Going back to her room, she changed into a swimsuit and then stalked out into the courtyard to dive cleanly into the pool, completely ignoring the surprised look on Hugo's face. She stayed in the water for quite some time, trying not to let her mind dwell on the long day that lay ahead. Somehow she would get through it—somehow, and early tomorrow morning Carlos would come for her and then it would all be over. That thought gave her courage as she eventually climbed out and pushed her wet hair back from her face. Hugo was sitting in a garden chair, smoking a cigarette and watching her with a coiled spring alertness that she had come to recognise beneath his apparently casual demeanour.

'Just where do you think you're going?' he demanded as she went to walk past him.

'To fix myself some breakfast.'

'You'll wait until I say you can go. Sit down.' He gestured to a chair placed next to him, but Kate faced him defiantly.

'Why the hell should I? Just because you're holding me here with all the doors and windows locked it doesn't mean that you can order me about like some petty tyrant. I don't *have* to listen to you and I'm not going to. And you can stand there and threaten me with as much violence as you like,' she added as he came quickly to his feet, 'because I don't believe you'd use it. You may put on a big act to frighten me, but you're too civilised to resort to it, even if you wanted to. You didn't last night and I don't think you will now. And I. . . .' She broke off as Hugo took one unhurried step towards her, his eyes dangerous.

'So you think I'm too civilised to use violence, do you? I see I shall have to give you a demonstration.' He reached out suddenly to put his hand in the small of her back and pushed her in the pool, jumping in beside her a second later. As Kate came up and tried to look round, he wound his hand in her hair and pushed her under again, holding her there. Desperately she tried to break loose, tearing at the hand that held her. She had been too taken by surprise to take a deep breath and soon she was fighting for air. At last he let her up, gasping and retching.

'So you still think you can defy me, do you?'

Kate took great lungfuls of air, her eyes full of antagonism when she looked at him. He saw it and deliberately pushed her down again. After the second time he hauled her out, letting her lie gasping on the side until she'd got her breath back a little.

'Now. Sit in the chair.'

Shivering violently despite the heat of the day, she managed to get to her feet, almost falling into the chair, pulling her legs up and wrapping her arms round herself, huddled into a small, vulnerable ball. She had never felt so frightened in her life, not even last night, when he had seemed overtaken by and out of control of his anger, had she been so frightened. He had coldbloodedly set out to show her just how much she was in his power and now there were no illusions left, he didn't care how far he went to make her do what he wanted.

'What is Simon Robertson to you? Why did he lend you this villa?'

'He's my solicitor. I went to him after I left you. He said I could stay here until—until things were sorted out.' Her voice came in broken, stilted sentences, the last five minutes of terror still too vivid in her mind for her to do anything but answer him.

'Is he your lover? How many times have you been to bed with him?'

'No, he's a friend.'

Then he went on: had she slept with Carlos, how many lovers had she had, had she ever given herself to any photographer or agent to further her career, had she ever been with a man for money?

Dully she answered no to all of them, but this last roused her a little from her apathy and she balled her hands into tight fists, but was too cowed to answer back.

'Why don't you admit that Leo Crawford is your

lover?' His voice was going on, softly and persuasively now. 'Most career women live with a man nowadays rather than have the ties of marriage and children—there's no shame to it. So you can tell me. All you've got to do is tell me and then you'll be free to go.'

But not until you've had your last pound of flesh, Kate thought miserably. She turned her head into the chair, not even listening any more. The knowledge that he hated her enough to treat her like this was a hard, suffocating ball inside her.

At last he stopped, realising that his voice had become monotonous and she wasn't listening properly. 'All right, you can go and get some breakfast now.'

Obediently she stood up and walked slowly back into the kitchen where she made herself prepare a proper cooked meal of scrambled eggs on toast. She felt better after she had eaten, only an occasional shiver betraying the traumas of the last hour. Her hair was still wet, hanging heavily round her neck. From somewhere she found the courage to go out into the courtyard again and lie face down on a lounger, letting the sun dry her hair. Surprisingly she slept, and when she awoke she was amazed to find that Hugo had draped a towel over her to protect her from the fierce, burning heat of the midday sun. Rather stiffly she sat up and looked around her. Hugo was sitting at a garden table in the shade of the wall, writing a letter. He looked up when he heard her move, and their glances met and held. Kate felt her heart give a dizzying lurch and quickly looked away, her hands gripping the sides of the lounger. He had hurt her in every way, both physically and mentally, she ought to hate him more than anyone she'd ever hated in her life, despise him even for the way he'd treated her; but she didn't—how could she when she still loved him?

But Hugo mistook her quick avoidance of his glance for guilt. He came over and sat on a lounger beside hers, leaning back in it casually while he lit a cigarette. Then it started again, the endless catechism. She answered slowly, miserably, gazing at the sun reflected in the now still waters of the pool. Gradually she realised that a note of annoyance had entered his voice; she wasn't giving him the answers he wanted. Then from somewhere she realised that her strength lay in her complete innocence. He could ask all the questions he wanted and because she was telling the truth she could go on indefinitely, last out longer than he could. The thought brought her renewed optimism that must have shown in her voice, because after a moment he tried a new tactic. As he interrogated her he began to run his fingers lightly down her arm, then down her bare back, gently stroking her skin, his hand warm and sensuous.

Kate's voice faltered despite herself. His touch had always made her go to pieces. She tried desperately to control herself and managed to say with creditable steadiness, 'Take your hand off me.'

He did so at once, but when Kate looked at him she saw by the mocking smile on his lips that he knew he had got to her.

Standing up, he said, 'Go and get dressed. Put on an evening dress or something. We'll go out for a meal.'

'Do you really mean it?' she asked with an incredulous stare.

'I wouldn't have said it if I hadn't,' he replied brusquely.

Feeling stunned by his sudden volte-face, Kate used the bathroom and then went into her room to change. She couldn't understand why he was letting her out of the villa; he must surely realise that she would try to get away at the earliest opportunity. Perhaps he had some new trick up his sleeve, some new scheme to humiliate her in public. She had been applying her make-up, but that thought made her stop in the middle of putting on eye-shiner to disguise the dark circles under her eyes. Perhaps it would be better to refuse to go with him. At least in the villa she knew where she stood with him. But if she stayed there wouldn't be any chance at all of getting away, and what was more, Hugo would have the satisfaction of thinking her totally cowed and dispirited.

Pulling a dress of bronze-coloured, crinkled cheese-cloth over her head, Kate tried distractedly to think what to do. Was he taking her out so that he would have witness to the fact that they were together and so prevent her from getting an annulment? After all, they had spent the night together in the villa and of course there were no witnesses to the fact that they hadn't actually slept together, she thought bitterly. Her hair was a mess, but she brushed it till it shone and it had enough curl in it not to look too bad.

Her mind kept churning over ways and means of breaking free of him, rejecting most of them as being completely impossible almost as soon as she'd thought of them. But then she had an idea. Quickly she searched in her handbag for a pen and a piece of paper, then wrote a note asking the finder to send the police to the villa, adding that it was not a joke. This she folded into a small square and hid in her powder compact. She might not have to use it, but it was always useful to have an alternative plan.

Hugo took her to a nightclub on the coast, its low ceiling criss-crossed with beams, and the white-painted walls with arches leading from the bar to the restaurant giving it a Moorish effect. It was small and intimate with lighting that left the corners in shadow. Hugo spoke to the head-waiter in fluent Spanish and they were shown to a table in one of the corners that was on a slightly raised dais with a banister acting as a half-wall so that when they sat down she was hemmed in by the wall behind her, the wooden banister at one side, the table in front of her and Hugo on her other side. Neatly organised from his point of view, but not from hers.

They ate in uncompanionable silence. Gradually the place began to fill, mostly with local Majorcans by the look of them and obviously regular patrons, for they exchanged greetings and jokes with the head-waiter and other diners. There were also a few tourists who looked eagerly around, avid to soak up local colour. Kate was too tense to eat much, instead sipping the wine to give her the courage to make a break for it whenever an opportunity arose. After the meal Hugo ordered Sangria, a Spanish drink made with red wine and served in a large jug with slices of orange and lemon floating on the top among lumps of ice. A trio of two Spanish guitarists and a tambourine player, all men, came into the room amidst shouts of applause. They were dressed in a uniform of sorts, tight white jeans and blue cotton shirts. The two guitarists were Spaniards and were extremely good, but the tambourine player was a fair-haired European who also sang in a variety of languages. They were versatile and had the trick of getting their audience with them, so that soon everyone was joining the singing and swaying to the music.

But Kate couldn't relax; she was tense with expectancy and kept lifting her glass to drink, she was so nervous that she had to do something with her hands because they were shaking so much. For the same reason she also kept playing with the clasp of her evening bag, a habit she had when nervous. It seemed no time at all before the jug of Sangria was empty and Hugo called the waiter over to order another. While he was giving the order, Kate stood up.

'I'm just going to the cloakroom,' she said quickly and moved to squeeze past the table and hurry out of a side door.

But Hugo was right behind her. 'Oh, no, you don't!'

She turned on him indignantly. 'Look, I'm not trying anything. I need to go to the ladies' room.' Bravely she tried to brazen it out.

'All right, I'll wait for you outside.' He took her arm and escorted her to the cloakroom. She went to go inside, but he stopped her again. 'I'll take care of this for you,' and he plucked the bag from her hand.

Trying to keep her voice even, she protested, 'But I need it. I want to put on some lipstick.'

'So that you can write a message on the mirror? I don't think so.' He opened her bag and took out her lipstick, taking off the cap and examining it before handing it to her. 'You can put it on here.' He opened the compact and the piece of paper fell out. 'Pick it up.'

Slowly she did so, feeling sick. He read it, then screwed it up and put it in his pocket, watching her with contemptuous amusement as he did so, knowing by the sagging of her shoulders how defeated she felt.

Afterwards they returned to their table and gradually Kate realised despairingly that she hadn't stood a chance of getting away from him; he was as much in control of her now as at the villa. Even if she stood up and shouted for help, he would merely tell people that she was either drunk or ill and carry her out. So why had he brought her here? Moodily she drank more of the potent drink; at least it helped to deaden the hurt. The trio were singing again, less rousing songs now that it was getting late and everyone was pleasantly tired and slightly tipsy. They went towards one of the customers, a tall, middle-aged man, and seemed to be asking him to sing. He was obviously a popular regular, for as soon as they saw them, all the other people joined in, clapping their hands and calling encouragement. At last the man raised his hands in a gesture of submission and came to stand in the cleared space in the centre of the floor. Several more lamps were turned out so that he stood in a pool of soft, amber light, and the audience immediately quietened, waiting, expectant. One of the guitarists began to play gently in the background and then the man began to sing. It was *Granada*, the song beloved by Spaniards and foreigners alike, and he sang it remarkably well, his voice filling the little club with melody and lifting the spirit out into the night, across the sea and the plains and up into the high Sierras.

When he was done there was a prolonged, awesome silence and then a storm of clapping as everyone got to their feet to cheer, or banged the tables and shouted, 'Bravo!' In the midst of it Hugo touched Kate's arm and indicated that he wanted to leave. For a moment there was rebellion in her eyes, but then she saw his face tighten and she came, slowly and reluctantly, to her feet and let him lead her out.

Arriving back at the villa, Hugo left his car round the side and opened the door for her to go in. Kate paused in the doorway, inhaling her fill of the scented air, perfumed with jasmine and bougainvillaea from the shrubs that grew against the walls and ran riot over the roof. It was going to be hell to be shut in that small room again after the brief glimpse of freedom. Perhaps that was why he had done it, hoping that she would do anything rather than spend another night in those airless conditions. Well, if that was so then he was doomed to disappointment. Resolutely she lifted her chin and walked straight through to her room, closing the door firmly behind her.

She undressed and put on a new sleeveless, knee-length nightshirt with slits up the sides, hoping that it might be a bit cooler than a full-length nightdress. Turning off the light, she pulled back the cover. Something leaped from the bed and landed in her hair. Kate screamed and tried frantically to shake it out. The light snapped on as Hugo ran in, dressed in a navy bathrobe.

'What's the matter?'

'There was something in the bed. It jumped in my hair. Oh, get it out, please. I can feel it!' She shook her head violently in an attempt to shift it, but she could feel the thing running across her neck.

Quickly Hugo came behind her and picked it off. 'It's all right, it's only a cricket. Ugly brutes, I admit, but quite harmless.'

He took it to let it loose outside and then came back to where she was feverishly searching the bed to make sure there weren't any more of the beastly things.

'It must have got in when we had the door open this afternoon.' He came to put his hands on her arms. 'You're shaking.' Gently he began to rub her arms.

'I have this thing about insects crawling on me. I just can't stand it,' she told him unevenly. She remembered how it had felt and shivered violently.

Hugo drew her closer to him and put his hands on her back, massaging it with smooth even strokes. Kate shut her eyes and felt the tremors slowly die away. His hands were firm and yet infinitely soothing. She leant her head against his shoulder, and for a while it was just as it had been before the wedding and she felt all her cares and unhappiness evaporate away. Gradually his hands moved further, began to caress her hips and her thighs. She made a little sound deep in her throat and moved sensuously against him. Hugo's mouth came down to seek hers, exploring her lips with little kisses that promised everything, then deepened with passion as he pulled her hard against him.

For a few minutes she was lost in his embrace. Brokenly she murmured his name, then stood very still as realisation came flooding back. She disengaged herself and stepped away, an infinite sadness in her eyes.

'Please go now, Hugo.'

'Go? Now?' He stared at her, a fierce hunger in his face, his jaw taut. 'My God, you're as hard as nails. Do you really expect me to just walk away after this?'

'Yes, I do. Because you said that you'd only take me if I was willing. Well, I'm not, I want you to go.' Her voice sounded quite calm, but it was a far cry from what she was feeling.

'No, you don't. Whatever you pretend, the way you

responded just now proved that you want me as much as I want you, so why don't you admit it?'

'I do. I've never said that I didn't.' Kate gave a bitter smile at the amazed look in Hugo's eyes.

'Then why ... ?'

'I might want you, but I won't give myself to you. You see, it's really quite simple; I'll never give myself to a man unless he loves me—and you don't, you never have. You just let me think you did because you knew it was the only way you would ever get me. But I found out the truth in time. And now I hate you so much that I'll never give....'

She took a hasty step back as Hugo came quickly to take hold of her. 'You don't hate me,' he said softly. His hands moved to cup her breasts, his fingers moving rhythmically against the thin material of her night-shirt. 'You just hate yourself because I can make you feel this way.' He undid the buttons down to her waist and his hands moved inside, his touch rousing her against her will so that her body hardened under his hands. He gave a small sound of triumph, confident that she could no longer resist him, and Kate turned her head away, tears of humiliation at his cold-blooded handling running silently down her cheeks.

Slowly he slipped the nightshirt off her shoulders. A tear trickled on to his hand and only then did he look up. For a long moment he was quite still, then, 'By God,' he swore savagely, 'you pull every trick there is in the book!' And then he was gone, striding swiftly from the room, leaving Kate to pull her nightshirt back on and sink to a huddled heap on the floor.

CHAPTER SEVEN

KATE knew that she had to be awake early the next morning so that she would be ready when Carlos came and so she only dozed fitfully, waking in the early hours in a panic in case she'd overslept and then unable to go to sleep again, worrying about what would happen. By six she was fully dressed, her cases packed, her ears pricked for the first sound of a car. She thought that Hugo must be still asleep after their evening at the nightclub, but she was afraid to venture past his room in case she woke him. By six-thirty she couldn't stand staying in the bedroom any longer and crept quietly out into the corridor. He was lying on his back, bars of sunlight through the slats of the shutters gilding the smooth skin of his bare chest and accentuating the strong planes of his face. But in his sleep there was a look of vulnerability about his mouth that was never there when he was awake, a softening of his features that hinted at the man within the hard outer veneer he showed to the world.

For a long moment Kate studied him. Last night he had so shamed and humiliated her that he had driven her to the mortification of letting him see her cry, something which she had thought she had too much pride ever to do. But in that had been her salvation, because she was quite sure that if she hadn't wept he would have taken her, taken her without love, compassion, or tenderness, exulting only in his possession of her at last, his power to degrade her into becoming the thing he accused her of; a woman without morals who would give herself to him just to satisfy the need he aroused in her.

Abruptly Kate turned and went into the kitchen. It was a forlorn hope, but she tried both the kitchen and front doors anyway. They were both locked and the keys removed. There might have been just a chance that he had forgotten to lock one of them after coming back from the nightclub. Nervously she glanced at her watch: six-forty-five. Carlos should be here at any minute. Crossing to the front window, she tried to peer out through the shutters to the main road, eyes straining to catch a glimpse of his car.

But it had already turned into the track leading to the farm before she saw it, the noise of the engine carrying clearly over the early morning air. Kate picked up a large ornamental vase, ready to throw it to smash the window as soon as Carlos came within earshot. The car was right up to the house now, but he hadn't turned off the engine yet. Oh, hurry, Carlos, hurry! she prayed silently. Then the engine cut out and she heard the car door opening. She lifted the vase above her head in both hands and prepared to hurl it at the window as Carlos' footsteps sounded on the gravel outside.

The vase was wrenched suddenly from her hands as Hugo came up behind her. He sent her sprawling across the settee and then came to hold her and silence her as Carlos knocked loudly on the door. But first Hugo had to set the vase down and in those seconds Kate had time to scream for help at the top of her voice, hoping against hope that Carlos would hear through the thickness of the shutters. The scream was cut off abruptly as Hugo's hand came over her mouth. But it was too late, Carlos had heard. He began to hammer on the door and call her name and then, finding it locked, to throw his weight against it.

With a muttered curse Hugo let her go. He was wearing only slacks and an open shirt, his hair still tousled from sleep. Angrily he took in the fact that she was dressed for travelling and said furiously, 'You little cheat, you knew someone was coming. Who is he?'

The light of victory in her eyes, Kate retorted, 'It's Carlos. He's called to take me to the airport. I'm flying back to England today, away from you and your twisted egotistical need for retribution!' She pulled out of his hands and ran to the door. 'Carlos, help me! It's the man from the nightclub, he's holding me prisoner. Get the poli....' Surprise made her break off in mid-sentence as she saw Hugo's hand come past her to insert the key in the lock and then turn it.

'Well, aren't you going to let him in?' he said coolly.

For a moment she was too startled to move, could only stare stupidly at the grey eyes that looked back at her so sardonically, but then she had turned the handle and thrown the door open to project herself into Carlos' arms and cling tightly to him, unable to think of anything but the relief of being free.

'Hallo there. Come on in. You must be Carlos de Halmera. Kate's told me a lot about you. I'm Hugo Merrion, by the way—Kate's husband.'

Dimly she heard Hugo speaking, but this last made her head come up with a jerk. She saw the startled look in Carlos' eyes and said quickly, 'No, that isn't true. Oh, please, Carlos, take me away! He was waiting here for me when you brought me from your house. Oh, God, it's been a nightmare!'

'You say this man has been holding you here against your will?' The amazement in his voice started to change to anger.

'Yes, for two days. He....'

'Look, why don't you come inside and let me explain. I'm afraid Kate is overwrought at the mome....'

'No, don't listen to him,' Kate broke in hysterically. She gripped the lapels of Carlos' jacket, almost shaking him in her frantic need to get away and half dragging him towards the car. 'Just get me away from him, Carlos. Now!'

'But if he has been holding you here, if he has hurt you in any way, then the police must be informed—but I've a few things to say to him first.' Furious on her behalf, Carlos put Kate in the passenger seat of his car and then turned purposefully back towards Hugo, belligerently tightening his fists. 'You animal! What have you done to her?'

Hugo leaned negligently against the post supporting the porch, arms folded, making no attempt to defend himself. 'What my wife and I do when we're alone together is none of your damn business,' he said curtly.

Carlos stopped short. 'Your wife? I don't understand.' Then, 'Don't think you can trick me that way. Kate told me at the nightclub that she'd never seen you before.'

'She lied to you.' Hugo shrugged his shoulders regretfully. 'I'm sorry to have to say it about my own wife, but there it is—she lied.'

'But why? Why should she lie? And why do you say

again that she is your wife?' Poor Carlos was becoming completely bewildered.

'Because she is. We were married only two weeks ago. If you don't believe me I can show you the marriage certificate,' he added. 'It's in my wallet.' He straightened up and walked calmly to the car to lean his hands on the roof and look mockingly through the open window at Kate before turning back to Carlos. 'Unfortunately all the fuss and excitement of getting married caused Kate to have a slight nervous breakdown. She couldn't face up to it, so she ran away, tried to pretend that it hadn't happened. Voluntary amnesia, I think the psychiatrists call it. Naturally I followed her here and tried to take her back so that she could be treated. But I hoped that by keeping her here quietly for a while she could rest and recover. And in fact. . . .'

'That isn't true! None of it!' Kate was out of the car and had run round to Carlos, again pulling him towards the vehicle. 'Oh, Carlos, can't you see that he's lying to you? He screwed down the windows and the shutters so that I couldn't get away. And he's been going on and on at me all the time, trying to make me. . . .' She stopped, biting her lip, aware that her voice was rising hysterically. 'Carlos, just take me away from here, please. I promise I'll explain everything to you later, but now just please let's go away!'

'Don't you think you ought to see the marriage certificate first?' Hugo broke in evenly, adding, 'After all, you *would* be abducting my wife.'

Slowly Carlos put his hands on her shoulders, looking searchingly into Kate's face. 'Kate, is he telling the truth? Are you his wife?'

A hunted look came into her eyes and she looked away, knowing that she had to lie to him, but hating to have to do it. 'N-no.' She tried to say it firmly, but she only made it sound mumbled. Cheeks flaming, she looked up and saw that he hadn't believed her. Desperately she tried to cover up and convince him. But by then it was too late, because Hugo had gone swiftly to his room and come back with his wallet.

'Here's the certificate.' He held a folded paper out to Carlos.

Before he could look at it, Kate burst out, 'All right! So what if I am married to him? What difference does it make? Carlos, I'm appealing to you, I'm *begging* you to take me away from him. From a man who doesn't love me or care about me. I'll tell you why I ran away from him; because I found out that all he wanted was my body. He just wanted to own me, possess me, and he....'

'But as your husband he has the right,' Carlos broke in, his face a bewildered mixture of doubt and uncertainty.

'No, he has no rights over me if I don't choose to give them. And he killed everything between us when he....'

But Hugo had come up to her, interrupting to say solicitously, 'Darling, you're getting overwrought again. Please try to keep calm.' He pulled her against his chest so she couldn't speak. Over her shoulder he said to Carlos, 'She was getting much better. Only last night she was well enough for me to take her out to a restaurant for a meal. It was the Copacabana, do you know it?'

'Why, yes. You went there last night?' Carlos' voice sounded even more bewildered. 'But Kate said you kept her prisoner and....'

'I know what she said, but as I told you, the poor girl's been ill. But with rest and nothing to excite her I'm sure she'll soon be well again.'

By exerting all her strength Kate managed to free herself and glared at Hugo balefully. 'My God, you hypocritical swine!' Desperately she turned to Carlos. 'You once said you owed me a greater debt than you could ever repay for saving your sister when she was going to jump the hedge and the harrow was in the way. Carlos, repay that debt now. Don't even think about anything that he's told you. Just listen to me and believe me when I say I'm very, very sane. And all I want you to do is to take me to the airport and put me on a plane to England just as we arranged. Please, Carlos, I have the right to ask you to do this for me.'

He stared at her for long moments, the play of emotions obvious in his face. Behind her Hugo stood tensely silent while she gazed imploringly into Carlos' eyes. That he wanted to help her and to repay the debt she demanded of him was clear, but against it was the centuries of traditional upbringing that decreed that a woman's place was by her husband's side. And perhaps the victory he had so narrowly won over Consuelo played a part in his decision, because at last he said slowly, '*Lo siento*, Katerina. I'm sorry, but I can't take you away from your husband.' And she knew that she had lost.

She stood silently in the driveway, not looking at him, her head bent in despair. He reached out to touch her shoulder, almost as if asking her forgiveness, but

Kate hardly felt it. He walked towards the car, then stopped and came back.

'I forgot. I collected a letter from your postbox for you.'

He held it out to her, but Hugo came and took it from him and put his hands on her shoulders. 'I'll look after it for her, shall I? And please don't worry about Kate, she'll be well taken care of.'

'You'll write and let me know how she is?'

'Of course.'

And then Carlos was in his car and driving away down the track. As if his going had galvanised her back to life, Kate suddenly shook off Hugo's hands and started to run after the car. But it was much too fast for her and she tripped and fell to her knees in the dust as she watched it turn into the main road and pull away.

Hugo didn't hurry any when he came after her. Strolling up, he looked down at her as she still knelt on the ground, gazing hopelessly after the car, before stooping to pick her up and carry her back to the house. Once there, he carried her into the kitchen and set her down in a chair by the table. Kate leaned her elbows on the table and put her head in her hands, feeling utterly defeated. She had pinned all her hopes on Carlos rescuing her from Hugo, and now he too had let her down. Now she had no hope left, nothing. She was completely at Hugo's mercy, not that he would be weak enough to ever show her any, she realised with bitter cynicism.

He came now to put his hand in her hair and jerk her head back so that she had to look up at him as he towered menacingly over her.

'All right, you managed to hold out till now because you knew that Halmera was coming. But now you know the truth, don't you? No one's going to help you now. You're going to stay here with me until you give me what I want, and there isn't one person in the world who gives a damn what happens to you. Do you understand, Kate, do you? There's just the two of us alone here together. Just you and me.' There was a vicious edge to his voice which made Kate cringe away from him. When he saw it he laughed triumphantly and she realised that he thought her completely intimidated and broken.

But when one is in desperate trouble there is sometimes a desperate remedy. He wanted two things from her: the details of her supposedly immoral life-style, and for her to give herself to him willingly. But there was just a chance that if she made the first sound sordid and repugnant enough he might be so disgusted that he would want nothing more from her. It was a small and miserable hope to cling to and one from which she cringed inwardly, but it was all she had left, the conviction that Hugo would be too fastidious to touch the kind of person she had to try to make herself out to be.

Putting on the act of one's life in such circumstances, and making Hugo believe in it, wasn't going to be easy, but she must force herself to do it. Deliberately she straightened in the chair and said in apparent submission, 'All right, what do you want to know?'

For a moment he was still, as if he couldn't really believe that he'd won at last. 'Just a minute.' He went into his bedroom and came out carrying a plastic bag, the sort you get in duty-free shops. He went behind her and she heard the chink of glasses as he took two from the shelf just behind her chair, then he set the glasses and a bottle of cognac on the table together with a fresh pack of cigarettes and an ashtray. Nothing like making yourself comfortable, Kate thought cynically.

He sat down opposite her and poured out the drinks, pushing one towards her. She shook her head and he shrugged. 'Suit yourself.' Before he asked the first question he lit a cigarette and leant back, watching her through the smoke. Kate tried to school her face into a look of sulky defeat. 'All right, so now I want the truth, the whole truth. Do you understand?'

Silently she nodded.

'Is the man you shared a flat with, Leo Crawford, your lover?'

Kate took a deep breath and crossed her fingers under the table in a sudden reversion to childish habit. 'Yes.'

'For how long?'

'Several years—I knew him before I came to London.'

'Was it his idea that you married me?'

'That I got a rich husband, yes. It didn't matter who,' she added insultingly.

Hugo's fingers tightened on his cigarette. 'To what purpose?'

Kate shrugged. 'I'm expensive. We decided I needed a husband to keep me, pay my bills.'

'I offered to do that for you when I wanted to make you my mistress.'

'Yes, but you'd hardly be willing to share me with another man. You'd have dropped me as soon as you found out that Leo and I were—getting together every time your back was turned. It takes longer to get a divorce and I would have been able to get maintenance and alimony,' she said, improvising quickly.

'Why me?'

'You just happened to come along first.' She saw a muscle tighten in his jaw and suddenly knew with an exultant feeling that she was getting through to him, that she had the power to hurt him. That it was nothing more than his pride that was being wounded was obvious, but it might be enough—it *had* to be enough. But it would take much more yet. 'If it hadn't been you it would have been some other dupe.'

'Is Crawford the only lover you've had?' he snapped at her, then, at the look on her face, he leaned forward and caught her wrist. 'How many, Kate? How many have there been?'

She managed to make her voice sound hard and sneering. 'Who's counting? He wasn't the first—and he definitely won't be the last.'

'Who was the first? Answer me!' he ordered when she hesitated.

'All right, I'm trying to. He was some boy I met at school. He promised to take me to a pop concert so long as I let him do what he wanted.'

'How old were you?'

She shrugged and looked away. 'Fifteen, nearly sixteen.'

The grip on her wrist tightened momentarily and then he thrust her hand away as if he were in contact with something dirty and infectious. 'So you were selling yourself even at that age. How many others have you given yourself to for—favours?'

Kate thought it was time she showed some defiance. 'Mind your own business!'

Her untouched drink went flying as he lunged towards her. 'You'll tell me, you little slut. You'll tell me if we have to stay here all day and all night! Now, how many times have you sold yourself?'

Kate winced inwardly. The pig! Well, she could hurt back too. 'All right! You want to know the truth —well, I'll give it to you. I sold myself as often as it was necessary. To get contracts and assignments and for clothes, or just to get my hair done for free. And I've even done it for money! Yes, that shocks you, doesn't it?' she added contemptuously when she saw him flinch as if he'd been hit. 'But there's nothing I wouldn't do to get what and where I want. Fat men, old ugly men, and even supercilious swine like you; I don't give a damn who they are or what they are so long as I get what I want!'

She went to go on, but Hugo came to his feet suddenly, his face white and pinched, a look of sickened abhorrence in his eyes. 'All right, I've heard enough!' He looked at her with utter loathing, as if she was something repulsive and ugly. No one had ever looked at her like that before.

Kate sat there shaking, the effort it had cost her only now taking effect and leaving her feeling weak, her nerves in shreds. She hardly took any notice as Hugo went behind her, but then he placed something on the table just out of her reach. Dully she looked up and saw that it was a small portable cassette recorder. She suddenly became very still, slowly raising her eyes to look into his.

'I got it from my room when I fetched the cigarettes and drink. It recorded every word.' To emphasise his point he wound the tape back a little way and then pressed the Play button so that she heard her last sentences carry clearly across the stillness between them.

Wretchedly she turned her head away. 'I intend to use it, to ruin you and your boy-friend. Life is going to be extremely unpleasant for you for a long time to come, and you're going to wish to God that you'd never....'

Abruptly Kate stood up, unable to bear any more. 'But at least I'll be free of you. And that makes it worth it, because I hate you! I hate you more than anyone I've ever known in my life!' And she ran out of the room and left him standing alone, grimly looking after her.

CHAPTER EIGHT

KATE didn't know how long it was after she had run into the sitting-room and thrown herself on to the settee that she finally noticed that the front door wasn't shut properly. Hugo had kicked it shut behind him when he'd carried her inside, but it wasn't completely closed. And then she saw that the key was still in the lock. She rather thought that her ruse had worked and that Hugo would have no more to do with her, but she wasn't going to hang around to be subjected to any more insults when there was a chance of getting away.

Hardly daring to breathe, she crept to the door and silently drew the key from the lock, one eye on the door leading to the kitchen in case Hugo came out, but he was still in there, seemingly almost stunned by her revelations. The hinges creaked only slightly as she pulled the door open just the few inches she needed to slip through, but the noise sounded like thunderbolts to her nerve-racked mind. But then she was through and forcing herself to lock the door behind her before running for the garage at the side of the house. As quietly as she could she opened the doors wide and then got into Simon's car. Thank heavens she'd left the keys in the ignition the last time she'd used it. There were long terrifying seconds while she again sorted out the unfamiliar controls, but then she'd found the choke and turned on the ignition. Mercifully it fired first time, the noise of the engine reverberating like a dozen pneumatic drills in the confined space of the garage, but then she was accelerating down the driveway, stones flying up from under the skidding wheels as she fought to control the car before turning into the main road. Glancing in the mirror as she did so, she caught a glimpse of Hugo running round from the back of the villa; he must have gone into the courtyard and jumped down from the wall to have got round there that quickly. But he was too late, too late! she thought exultantly. He could never hope to catch her now and this time it was his turn to be left behind in the dust.

Putting her foot hard down on the throttle, she shot down the road, but after screaming the tyres round a couple of bends she slowed down considerably, afraid of not being able to control it properly. An overwhelming sense of relief filled her, but with it came such an anguished feeling of dejection and despair that she had to clutch the steering wheel tightly and bite her lip hard to keep a hold on her emotions. But despite her efforts tears welled into her eyes and spilled down her cheeks. Angrily she brushed them aside and tried to concentrate on her driving. Only another mile or so to the village now.

Automatically she glanced in the mirror and stiffened as she saw a car coming up fast behind her. It looked vaguely familiar, but she couldn't think where she'd seen it before. Then it hit her; it was the car Hugo had hired! She'd been in such a hurry to get away that she'd completely forgotten it was still parked on the other side of the villa. And now Hugo was coming after her. Fear made her hands go slack and the car veered wildly across the road, but the sudden fright it gave her made her come to her senses and she hastily brought it back on the road and put her foot on the accelerator. If she could just get to the village before he caught her up. There would be people there to help her, perhaps even a police station.

Frenziedly she looked in the mirror again; he was only a couple of hundred yards behind now and closing fast, the far more powerful engine covering the distance between them far faster than she could get away. They were almost at the village now and she was already pulling on to the narrow strip of land that lay between the two halves of the sheer-sided quarry and acted as a bridge for the road. It wasn't far now, only another half mile. Oh, please let me make it, she begged. But then a horn sounded right behind her and when she glanced to the right she saw the other car alongside and trying to overtake her so that Hugo could force her to stop. Desperately she pushed the accelerator into the floor, knuckles white as she gripped the wheel, and managed to draw ahead a little, the speedometer far over to the right.

The horn sounded again, angrily. Kate rounded a slight bend with a clump of shrubs and bushes clinging to the roadside and saw the village. And also a tanker lorry, its red danger flag streaming out as it came fast towards her. Immediately towards her, in the same lane, because she had completely forgotten where she was and was driving on the left-hand side of the road! And Hugo was alongside her on the right, completely cutting off any hope of evading a smash with the lorry or of plunging off the road down into the stone floor of the quarry, fifty feet below.

With a sob of pure terror, Kate tried to brake, but it

was much too late—the lorry was only twenty yards away. Then suddenly she heard the sound of the horn again from her right and when she looked she saw that where Hugo's car had been there was only a blank space. Instinctively she threw the wheel hard over. Then she was past, within inches of the huge, thundering tyres of the tanker, as it roared by, its brakes screeching as the driver tried to bring it to a halt.

Kate somehow pulled up further down the road, feeling dizzy and sick, her nerves raw and palpitating, hardly able to believe that she was still in one piece. She opened the door and almost fell out into the road, her legs too weak to support her. The tanker, too, had come to a stop and the driver and his mate were running towards Hugo's car. For a moment she couldn't see why, but then she saw the car sway and realised that it was balanced precariously on the edge of the quarry, with one wheel hanging over the sheer drop below. She began to run then, fear putting strength back into her limbs. Oh, God, please don't let him go over! When she got there the men had got the door nearest them open. Hugo was sprawled unconscious across the seat and there was blood on his forehead where it had hit the windscreen.

'Get him out! Why don't you get him out?' Kate yelled at the men, forgetting that they probably didn't understand a word of English.

She tried to push past them to reach Hugo, but one of them pulled her back. He took her arm and pointed down into the car. Hugo's foot was wedged behind one of the pedals.

'A rope? Don't you have a rope?'

Desperately she mimed towing the car back on to the

road, but they shook their heads, waving their arms about and shouting Spanish at her that she couldn't understand until she wanted to scream. Then the smaller man inched his way into the car to try to free Hugo, but he had to get right over the wheel that was hanging over the edge and the car began to creak and sway, sliding slightly further over the edge when he got further in. Quickly he sprang back.

Kate realised that there was only one thing to be done. She indicated to the two men that they go to the back of the car and put their weight on it to try to balance it while she tried to free Hugo herself. They shook their heads and demurred at first, but when they saw that she was going ahead anyway, they reluctantly did as she wanted.

Slowly Kate crawled into the car, keeping her body as evenly spread out as she could. Hugo was wearing rope-soled canvas lace-ups and she hoped that if she could just get his shoe off she might then be able to release his foot. Gingerly she stretched her hands forward to try to reach it. Above her, Hugo groaned as he came to. He stirred and then reached for the wheel to pull himself up. As his weight came over the car began to dip again.

'Hugo, don't move! Just keep still, perfectly still,' Kate said urgently, desperately.

'Kate? What—what is it?'

'The car's in a—in a rather dodgy position, but if you just keep still for a moment we'll be able to get you out.'

She tried to speak calmly, to reassure him, but he must have heard the fear in her voice because he looked out of the window and said, 'Good God!' Then,

'Kate, get out of here. Do you hear me, get out of here at once.'

'Just as soon as your foot's free. Can you move it yourself, do you think?'

He tried, but it was wedged firmly. 'No, Kate, please. Leave me and go for help.'

Not bothering to answer him, she inched her way further in and began to untie his shoelace and then ease the shoe off his foot, but it was so tightly held that she had to exert all her strength to get it free. At last it came off, suddenly, so that she was jerked forward and the car began to sway again.

'Kate, get out!' Hugo yelled at her.

Too frightened to move, Kate could only keep perfectly still, praying that they wouldn't go over. She could hear the tanker driver calling out to her urgently, but she refused to take any notice. At last the swaying stopped and she said breathlessly, 'Can you get your foot out now if I help you?'

She reached forward again to lift the pedals and after a struggle Hugo managed to pull his foot clear. Kate felt a great wave of relief. Quickly she moved backwards across the floor, calling out to the two men. The Spaniards ran round to take Hugo by the shoulders and drag him clear just as the car began to skew and slide further towards the edge now that their balancing weight was removed. Kate waited until they got him clear and then threw herself out, grabbing at a bush to stop herself rolling over the edge. The car teetered for a long moment at the point of balance and then went over, falling almost gracefully until it crashed on its nose and burst into a great, roaring ball of flame.

Slowly, mechanically, Kate picked herself up and

went over to where they had laid Hugo in the grass at the side of the road. He had passed out again. One of the men ran to fetch her car, making her understand that he would drive them to the hospital. She nodded, glad to let them take over, her whole mind consumed by the anxiety that Hugo might be badly hurt. He didn't come round again until they were on the outskirts of Palma and approaching the hospital. Kate was sitting with him in the back seat, supporting his head on her shoulder. He opened his eyes and tried to say something, but bit his teeth together as a stab of pain hit him.

'Don't try to talk. We're nearly at the hospital.'

'Kate.' Her name was little more than a whisper, so that she had to lean close to him to hear. 'Don't—don't leave.' His hand came up to grip her wrist where she held him and then fell back loosely again as he sank back into oblivion.

The wait at the hospital seemed interminable. They had taken Hugo away as soon as they had arrived, leaving her to sit in a corridor to grow steadily more worried and anxious. Then a policeman had come to ask her questions about the accident, the tanker driver having already given his version of what had happened. They wanted to see her passport and when she couldn't produce it and refused to leave the hospital to go back to the villa with them to get it, they became suspicious that she might be drunk or high on drugs. But when she told them the simple truth, that she'd quarrelled with her husband, had run away and he'd come after her, they immediately became much more friendly; evidently what one did during the passion of a lovers' quarrel was excusable to the hot-

blooded Spaniards. They warned her that she would be
held responsible for the accident and then departed
after expressing the hope that Hugo would soon be recovered.

And then she was left alone again, not even able to
think of what she was going to do, of going back to
England; all she could think of was Hugo's dead-white
face and his mouth clamped tight shut against the pain.
It was a long time before anyone came to tell her anything, and then it was a nun, a nursing Sister, who
came towards her.

'Señora Merrion?'

Kate came hastily to her feet. 'Yes? *Si?*'

'It is all right, *señora*, I speak English.'

'My husband? How is he?'

'He is well. There are no broken bones. He may have
a slight concussion from the blow on his head, and his
ankle is badly bruised. We will keep him here tonight
and you can come and take him home tomorrow.'

Relief engulfed her and she put a hand to her head,
swaying a little so that the nun put out a hand to
steady her. Then she realised that they expected her
to collect Hugo tomorrow. 'Oh, but I....' Kate broke
off; there was no point in telling the nun that she
wouldn't be in Majorca tomorrow.

'Your husband is awake now. He asks to see you.'

Eyes wide, Kate could only stare at the white-cowled
nun. 'He wants to see me? Are you sure?'

'Oh, yes.' The Sister smiled. 'He has not stopped asking for you since he recovered consciousness. He is in
St Augustine's ward on the second floor. And now if you
will excuse me, *señora*?'

'Of—of course. Thank you.' Kate stood and watched

her go, her mind in a whirl. All that mattered was that Hugo wasn't badly hurt, that he was going to be all right. The fear and anxiety that had been a tight knot in her chest slowly eased and she was able to think more clearly. Why did he want to see her? To threaten her again, tell her that she would never escape from the consequences of what he believed she'd done? she wondered bitterly. Well, no thank you, she'd had about as much as she could stand of that.

She walked out of the cool interior of the hospital into the hot sun. The car was parked nearby and she got into it and drove slowly and carefully back to the villa. Her mind felt totally disorientated and confused. She'd told Hugo that she hated him, and in that moment she probably had, but the terrified fear that had consumed her when she thought he might be killed, the overpowering need to save him no matter what the cost to herself, had shown her just how much she still loved him. No matter what he'd done to her, or how much he might try to hurt her in the future, she knew that she would always go on loving him, and no one but him, until the day she died.

The key was still in the front door of the villa, only the wide-open garage doors and the skid marks in the gravel giving any indication of her escape and Hugo's angry pursuit. Aimlessly she wandered round the rooms. Everything was just as they had left it; the cassette recorder with the cassette lying beside it still on the kitchen table where Hugo must have dropped it when he came after her, her cases packed ready because she had so confidently expected Carlos to take her away, and, in Hugo's room, the indentation in the pillow where he had lain and the pyjama trousers thrown down when he had hastily changed after hearing Carlos' car. Kate sat down on his bed and reached out to touch the pillow, then picked it up and held it close to her own face.

She sat there for a long time in utter dejection, not crying, not anything, but eventually she managed to pull herself together a little. After reconnecting the phone, she called the airline and explained that she had been delayed, and they switched her ticket to a flight leaving that evening. So now she had several hours to while away. Her first thought was to go straight to the airport and wait there, but then she realised that she couldn't just leave the villa in this state; it wouldn't be fair after Margie and Simon had been kind enough to lend it to her. The normality of clearing the place up helped a lot. She set the pool to drain and stripped the beds, throwing out the unused food and putting all the rubbish ready for the dustmen to collect. The screwdriver she found in a drawer in Hugo's room and went round unscrewing all the shutters and windows, trying to leave the place just as it was when she arrived.

The hardest part was packing Hugo's things. He had brought just one suitcase and a flight bag with him and she carefully folded his clothes and packed them in neatly. The cassette player and tape she put in his flight bag together with his razor and the things he would need overnight at the hospital. She could drop them in on her way to the airport. She supposed she ought to have wiped the tape clean or destroyed it completely. After all, it wasn't true, and had been forced out of her anyway. And Hugo would certainly use it to make her life as intolerable as he could, to go on hurting her just as long as he wanted, until there was no more satisfaction to be gained from ruining her life, or until she moved out of his reach, somewhere where she would be safe from his vindictiveness. Perhaps in Buenos Aires with Leo. But somehow she was sure that Hugo would find her even there, would find her and try to destroy them both. Kate bit her lip, trying not to think about the future, to concentrate only on what she was doing.

Finding a duster and broom in the cupboard, she set to work to clean the place out and leave it neat and clean. The ordinariness of the task acted like occupational therapy and she felt better after she had put the things away and seen the finished results of her handiwork. Glancing at her watch, she decided she might as well call a taxi now; it would take a little time for it to come from the town. After she had phoned, she washed and re-applied her make-up. Her face looked white and tired and there were dark smudges under her eyes that the make-up couldn't hide. She put the jacket of her pale blue linen suit on over the darker shaded blouse, and then went round turning off the water and electricity. The sails of the windmill came slowly to a halt; the pool was empty, the water no longer lapping against the blue tiles, instead it looked somehow bare and neglected.

Determinedly Kate shut the kitchen door and locked it, then carried all the cases through to the sitting-room ready to put them in the taxi. Restlessly she moved around, straightening a cushion or making a pile of the magazines she had bought, thinking that she would leave them here in case Margie wanted to read them the next time she came. As she did so she noticed that the newspaper she had bought at the same time was still among them, still folded open at the page containing the photograph of her and Hugo leaving the church. Slowly she knelt down on the floor, staring at the paper. She had been so happy then, and Hugo had looked.... Oh, how could he have looked at her like that? So proudly, so *lovingly*, when all the time he.... The tears that she had held so tightly in check began to run down her cheeks unheeded as she gave way to her unhappiness.

Vaguely she heard a car coming up the driveway and realised that the taxi had arrived. She groped in her pocket for a handkerchief but stopped with it half-way to her face as the door opened.

'Hugo!'

She stared in incredulous amazement as he stood in the doorway. He was leaning on a stick to take the weight off his injured ankle and there was a bandage round his head, starkly white against his dark hair. He looked at her searchingly, seeing the tears and the forlorn, hopeless look in her face. He moved slowly, haltingly towards her. Kate had been too stunned at seeing him to move, but now she got hastily to her feet and put a finger up to brush away all evidence of her tears. Hugo put out a hand as if to touch her and then lowered it again when she flinched away from him. He glanced down and saw the paper on the floor. He raised his head to look intently at her face.

'They—they told me at the hospital that they were going to keep you in until tomorrow,' she managed at last.

'I know. I dismissed myself.'

Her head came up to look at him quickly then. His

face was very pale, his mouth pinched into a hard, tight line. 'Oh, you shouldn't have done that,' she said impulsively. 'They said you might have concussion. You should rest.'

'I'm all right,' he answered impatiently. 'You didn't come and see me, so. . . .'

'You didn't really expect me to, did you?' Kate broke in heavily.

But he went on as if she hadn't spoken. 'So I came here to find you. I had to see you, Kate.'

'Why? So you could keep me here to go on hurting and humiliating me? Or was it to make sure that I hadn't wiped your precious tape clean? Well, you can stop worrying, it's still quite safe. Here, listen for yourself if you don't believe me!' She ran to his flight bag and pulled it open, dragging out the cassette player and jamming the tape into it. He had wound the tape back and first she heard his voice asking if Leo was her lover. Kate put her hands over her ears in anguish.

Hugo dropped the stick and limped across the room to get hold of her arms and try to pull her hands down. 'Kate, listen to me.'

'Why? Because you still want me to give myself to you? Is that what you're trying to tell me? That you won't be satisfied until you've got everything you want from me?' She had to shout over the noise of the cassette and he swore and reached behind her to turn it off. But she still continued to yell at him. 'Why turn it off? You know you love listening to it. I bet you're going to enjoy listening to it every day for the rest of your life! Well, go ahead and enjoy it, because that's all you're going to get out of me,' she said fiercely. 'I'll never give myself to you willingly, so if you want me, if you can bear to touch me, then you're going to have to take me by force! But somehow—but somehow I don't think you're in a fit state to do that right now.' And suddenly she found that she was laughing, laughing and crying at the same time so that she put her hands up to cover her face.

'Kate! Oh, Kate, don't. Please don't cry.' Hugo pulled her roughly into his arms, holding her tightly against him. Immediately she drew away from him and he loosened his hold on her. 'Look.' He turned her round and then reached out to the cassette. He pressed the buttons that wound the tape clean.

Disbelievingly Kate watched it for a few moments and then turned her head to look at him questioningly. 'I—I don't understand. You did everything to get that, you didn't care what you did to me. Why should you wipe it off—unless,' her voice hardened, 'unless you want me to go through it all again, is that it? What's the matter, wasn't it specific enough for you? Do you want me to describe every detail, every. . . .'

Her voice had risen wildly, but Hugo's cut across hers urgently. 'Stop it! Kate, you've got to listen to me.' He raised his hands to put them on her shoulders, but then his jaw tightened and he lowered them again. 'Kate, I. . . .' He stopped, seemingly groping for words, curiously at a loss. 'Kate, why did you risk your life to get me out of that car?'

Eyes widening in surprise, she replied unsteadily, 'Because it was my fault, of course. I'd been driving on the wrong side of the road. If you hadn't moved out of the way like you did, I would have smashed into the tanker.'

'And so you felt you had to save me; a man you

hated, who had submitted you to mental torture? Who'd kept you against your will until he'd finally broken you? Why should you want to save a person like that, Kate? Why?'

'You—you saved my life,' she answered slowly.

The urgency was back in his voice as he asked, 'And that was the only reason? Was it?'

'Yes. Yes, of course it was.' She tried to make her voice firm. 'What other reason could there possibly be?'

He looked at her tensely for a moment. 'I don't believe you, Kate. Just as I don't believe a word that was on that tape.'

Kate stared at him. 'You don't believe it? But I answered all your questions, told you everything you wanted.'

'Everything you thought I wanted to hear, you mean,' Hugo said grimly. 'Because you were so desperate, so afraid of me, that you knew I'd never believe anything else. You'd pinned everything on your Spanish friend helping you to get away from me and when he let you down you took the only course open to you—to make me despise you so much that I'd want nothing more to do with you, wash my hands of you completely. And God help me, it might have worked— if it hadn't been for two things.'

Kate found that she couldn't look at him, she stared down at her hands clenched into tight fists. Her heart began to beat painfully in her chest and she found it difficult to speak. 'What things?' she managed in little more than a whisper.

Hugo's voice was firmer now, more sure of himself. 'The first was a basic instinct that kept telling me you weren't the promiscuous type, however much to the contrary the circumstances looked, and regardless of how black a picture you'd painted of yourself. I just couldn't believe that you could have done all those things and still look untouched and as if life had wonderful things still to offer.' He paused, then added slowly, 'It's an instinct I've been fighting for a long time, ever since I got over the first shock of seeing that detective's report. I went a little mad then, said a hell of a lot of things in the heat of the moment. Afterwards I decided to have the report double-checked because more than anything in the world I didn't want it to be true. But then I found you'd bolted and realised you'd overheard everything, and in the rather warped frame of mind I was in just then that pointed only to your guilt. So I got angry, more angry than I've ever been in my life. I had reports of you going to the airport with a man who gave you money, and then of you living with Carlos de Halmera. It all seemed to tie up with the first report.

'I was determined to hurt you then, hurt you as much as....' He broke off and lifted his hand to his bandaged head for a moment, his mouth twisting. He turned and limped to a chair, stretching his injured leg out in front of him. It must have pained him considerably while he'd been standing on it all this time. Rather wearily he went on, 'The rest you know, only too well. I went on forcing myself to ignore that basic instinct. It was as if some devil was driving me on, compelling me to make you show yourself up as the slut you seemed to be. And even when you told me it wasn't true I couldn't believe you, perhaps I was afraid to even *let* myself believe in you again.' His voice sounded tired. 'I don't know. I only know that when I came to in that car and saw the danger we were in, the whole world suddenly righted itself again.' He smiled mirthlessly. 'A hell of a place to find out!'

Without raising her head, Kate said haltingly, 'You said there were two things. What was the second?'

Hugo didn't answer straightaway. He got up and moved to the window, staring out. When he turned towards her there was a curiously naked, vulnerable look in his face. 'That it didn't matter, none of it. Even if you had done everything you said you did, it didn't make any difference.'

'To—to what?' Kate's eyes stared at him out of a face gone suddenly paler than before.

'To the fact that I love you.' He saw the look of utter disbelief that flickered across her face and went on quickly, 'I admit that when I first met you I only wanted you as a mistress, but after that time we quarrelled.... I missed you so much it was like losing a part of me. I told myself that it was only sexual desire, concupiscence, that after we'd been to bed together a few times the need for you would gradually die away.' Heavily he went on, 'And I thought the only way I could get you was to marry you. But when we started going out together again everything changed. I began to realise just how much you meant to me, that you were the one girl in the world I wanted to spend the rest of my life with. I'd waited such a long time for love, Kate, that at first I didn't recognise it when it came along. And when I did, I could hardly believe my luck, it seemed too good to be true. By the time we got engaged I was so in love that I was afraid to let you see how deeply and passionately I cared for you. Afraid to show how much I needed you in case I scared you. You were so sweet, so innocent.'

Hugo stopped then, his mouth twisted in remembered torment. 'And then I got that report. On our wedding day!' He leaned forward and gripped the back of a chair, his knuckles white under his tanned skin. 'God, Kate, if you knew how that hurt! To have the love and trust you'd so recently given torn to pieces was like having a hand grenade explode in your face! I think—I think I must have gone slightly mad for a while.'

Again he put his hand to his face for a moment, then straightened and said bitterly, 'All I wanted then was to hurt you, as if by hurting you it would somehow ease the pain of what you'd done to me. So I came after you, and when I found you I acted like a brute, tormenting you until I made you hate me, made you so desperate to get away from me that you nearly got yourself killed!'

'Stop it!' Kate half raised her hands towards him and said miserably, 'Can't you see it isn't any use? It doesn't matter how you felt, or how I felt for that matter. Because there's nothing left. Everything that was good between us is dead and rotten. You killed it when you believed that report. Even if you love someone you can't build on a foundation where there's no trust, no faith. Even if we—if we went on with this marriage, it would never work. I'd only have to smile at another man and you'd think I was having an affair. You'd make both our lives intolerable until we....'

'No! Kate, that isn't so.' Hugo came quickly across to her, talking with bewildering urgency. 'It isn't dead.

It can't be or we wouldn't both be here. If you'd really hated me you'd never have risked your neck to get me out of that car. And if I hadn't loved you and been terrified of losing you I'd still be in the hospital. All right, I know that I was every kind of a mad fool, but, Kate, can't you see that me following you here in the first place was only because I couldn't bear to just let you go?' He put his hands on her shoulders and turned her round to face him, desperate to make her understand, taking courage when she didn't flinch away.

Forcefully he said, 'We started again once before and we can do it now. But this time there'll be no holding back. Nothing is going to get in our way, not pride or prejudice. We'll both know that there's nothing we can do to each other that will ever completely kill what we feel for one another. The basic chemistry's there and it's strong enough to weather any storms, conquer any setbacks.'

Hugo looked into her face searchingly, but when she didn't answer him, gave no response, he looked away dejectedly and took his hands from her shoulders. For a long moment neither of them moved, but then Kate gave a deep sigh, her mouth trembling.

'I—I don't know what to say.'

'Say nothing. Not yet. I've been a damned idiot, Kate, and I know that I don't deserve you, but I'm begging you to give us another chance. He looked at her intently, his eyes dark in his pallid face, but she deliberately avoided his gaze. He turned slowly, blindly away. He took two steps and then stumbled a little as he put weight on his injured ankle.

Instantly Kate was at his side, her arms reaching out to steady him, but instead of letting her help him,

Hugo caught her to him, pulling her roughly into his arms and holding her gently, although his fingers gripped tightly on her shoulder. He just stood there, his face buried in her hair, the feel of her in his arms.

'I can't live without you, Kate,' he said at length, his voice muffled.

Slowly she raised her head to look at him, her hand reaching up to touch his face, to trace the outline of his mouth with her fingertips. Compulsively he turned his head to kiss her hand, pressing his lips hard into her palm.

'Hugo,' she said at last, 'Leo Crawford is my. . . .'

His head snapped round. 'No! Don't go on. I told you, it doesn't matter any more. I don't want to know about him.'

'But you must. Hugo, he's my brother. My half-brother,' she amended. 'We both had the same mother but different fathers. He managed to get back to London just before the wedding, but then he was recalled almost immediately.'

'Your brother?' His grey eyes stared into hers, a light of understanding and wonderment gradually growing in them. 'But why on earth didn't you tell me? If you'd only. . . .'

'Because I was too proud, I suppose.' It was Kate's turn to confess. 'I was going to, but when I overheard what you said it didn't seem to matter any more. I couldn't bear to think that you didn't love me, so like a stupid idiot I let my first instincts take over and I ran.'

'Oh, God, what a hell of a mess!' Then he said, almost as if he were afraid to ask, 'But why have you told me now? Why, Kate?'

'Because I love you,' she said simply. 'Because I've gone on loving you no matter what you did to hurt me. Oh, Hugo, I'm as much to blame as you. If I hadn't behaved like a proud, masochistic fool, running away instead of staying to. . . .'

She was unable to go on as Hugo's mouth came down on hers, effectively silencing her, kissing her with a desperate longing. His lips found her neck, her throat, her eyes, telling her far more than words ever could, setting her body on fire with the urgency of his passion. He kissed her as he'd never kissed her before, holding nothing back, letting her know that she meant everything to him, all his self-imposed barriers down for ever. At last he raised his head, but continued to hold her as if he'd never let her go.

Indistinctly he said, 'Darling, I want you. I want you now.'

'B—but your head and your ankle? Surely you can't. . . .'

'Do you really think I'd let a little thing like a bump on the head get in the way now? Oh, Kate, I've waited so long for you. All my life.' He put his hands on either side of her face and kissed her again, his whole being concentrated in the intensity and hunger of his kiss, the need he had to make her completely, utterly his.

'Hugo,' she whispered eventually.

'Stop worrying,' he said huskily. 'There's nothing to be afraid of.'

'I'm not afraid, not really. Please look at me.'

He drew back his head, saw a tremulous smile on her lips, and sparkling, tear-filled eyes that were full of wonder and happiness. With hardly any explanation or apology, he had got the surrender he'd wanted with such anger and bitterness. But there was no anger in him now, only passion and tenderness and an immeasurable joy.

The shutters were thrown wide to the moonlight, the windows open to let the scent of the white-flowered jasmine drift into the bedroom. Beside her Hugo stirred and gently drew his arm from under her head, trying not to disturb her. But Kate was fully awake.

'What is it? Is your head aching?' she asked anxiously, immediately worried that he might be in pain from his injuries.

'No, I'm all right.' He leaned down and kissed the tip of her nose. 'I left my lighter in the pocket of my trousers.' He got out of bed and picked up the trousers from the floor, fishing in the pockets. 'Hallo, what's this?' He came back and switched on the bedside lamp. 'It's that letter Carlos brought up from the box for you. I'm afraid I just shoved it in my pocket and forgot all about it. Had too many other things on my mind at the time,' he added, able to smile about it now.

He lit a cigarette and passed her the letter. 'Don't you want to read it?'

Kate reached over to let her fingers run gently, exploringly down his chest from his jawline to his waist. 'You read it for me.'

Hugo ground out the cigarette. 'If you expect me to concentrate on anything else when you're doing that, you're over-optimistic, my girl. Come here.'

Teasingly she moved away. 'No, read the letter first.'

'First?'

'First.'

'Okay, you win.' Hugo started to tear open the envelope and Kate moved to lean her head against his shoulder. After he had opened it, Hugo put an arm round her, drawing her closer, his eyes full of love and triumph as he looked at her, a new serenity in his face. He couldn't resist kissing her again and it was several minutes before she drew away and he began to read.

'It's from someone called Margie. She says:

Dearest Kate, Your godsons are fine again now and crawling into every kind of mischief. Do you need any more money? I know Simon gave you some at the airport, but if you need more just phone and we'll transfer some to you.

There isn't much news to tell you, I'm afraid. Evidently that swine who fooled you into marrying him has managed to hush the whole thing up, because there's nothing about it in the papers. Simon wrote to him at once but he's heard nothing definite.

Kate, love, I know you're going to be mad at us, but Simon and I talked it over and we agreed that the only thing to do is to get in touch with your brother and ask him to come over here to sort this thing out. Although Simon will do everything he can, you need someone beside that husband of mine to see you through this and look after you. How I'd love to see Hugo Merrion's face when he finds out who Leo really is!

Keep your chin up, love. It will soon be safe to come back and get your annulment. Then you'll be free and you can put the whole thing behind you.'

When he'd finished reading there was a short, tense silence before Hugo said in bitter self-recrimination,

'Swine is right. Oh, Kate, how the hell can you even bear to have me touch you after what I've done to you?'

Kate reached out to take the letter from him, tearing it into pieces, some instinct warning her that the next few minutes could be crucial for them. 'Margie is an old friend and she's very partisan. And I think I can bear to have you touch me, especially as you were just now.' Then seeing that he still looked grim and with-drawn, she went on seriously, 'Darling, it's over, for-gotten. I forgave you utterly a long time ago.'

His eyes were dark with torment. 'But can I ever forgive myself?'

'You must if you want us to be happy together. We've got to forget the past and live only for the future. And it's going to be such a wonderful future. We've got all the time in the world.' She put out a finger to smooth the grim look from his mouth. 'You must promise me that you won't think about it again, not ever. Please, Hugo!'

He caught her finger between his teeth and bit it gently. 'All right, but it won't be easy.'

'Yes, it will. I'll make it easy, you'll see.' Then to change the subject and take the tormented look from his face. 'What shall we do tomorrow?'

His eyes immediately became laughing, mischievous. 'Why, this, of course.'

'And what is this?'

'This.' And he slid down to demonstrate just what he meant.

Harlequin® Plus

A WORD ABOUT THE AUTHOR

Sally Wentworth began her career in the world of publishing by landing a newspaper job in the busy Fleet Street district of London, England. She thoroughly enjoyed the hectic atmosphere and the feeling that she was part of an organization determined to be the first with news and tops in circulation.

When she married, she left London and moved with her husband back to the rural county of Hertfordshire, just north of London, where she had been raised. Here she worked for the publisher of a group of magazines.

But the day came when her own writing made its claim on her energy and time. She began evening classes in creative writing and wrote free-lance articles for a number of magazines. One more step brought her to full-length book writing: her husband took on some evening work and she used the hours alone to write her first Harlequin—*Island Masquerade* (Romance #2155), published in 1978.

There have been a good many Sally Wentworth books since that first one—happily for her readers, who may not realize that Sally writes each manuscript by hand, being a much faster thinker than a typist!

Yours FREE, with a home subscription to
SUPERROMANCE™·

Now you never have to miss reading the newest **SUPERROMANCES**... because they'll be delivered right to your door.

Start with your **FREE** LOVE BEYOND DESIRE. You'll be enthralled by this powerful love story...from the moment Robin meets the dark, handsome Carlos and finds herself involved in the jealousies, bitterness and secret passions of the Lopez family. Where her own forbidden love threatens to shatter her life.

Your **FREE** LOVE BEYOND DESIRE is only the beginning. A subscription to **SUPERROMANCE** lets you look forward to a long love affair. Month after month, you'll receive four love stories of heroic dimension. Novels that will involve you in spellbinding intrigue, forbidden love and fiery passions.

You'll begin this series of sensuous, exciting contemporary novels...written by some of the top romance novelists of the day...with four every month.

And this big value...each novel, almost 400 pages of compelling reading...is yours for only $2.50 a book. Hours of entertainment every month for so little. Far less than a first-run movie or pay-TV. Newly published novels, with beautifully illustrated covers, filled with page after page of delicious escape into a world of romantic love...delivered right to your home.

Enter a uniquely exciting new world with

Harlequin American Romance™

Harlequin American Romances are the first romances to explore today's love relationships. These compelling novels reach into the hearts and minds of women across America... probing the most intimate moments of romance, love and desire.

You'll follow romantic heroines and irresistible men as they boldly face confusing choices. Career first, love later? Love without marriage? Long-distance relationships? All the experiences that make love real are captured in the tender, loving pages of **Harlequin American Romances.**

What makes American women so different when it comes to love? Find out with **Harlequin American Romance!**

Send for your introductory FREE book now!